Praise for

"A Hollywood adventure that's truly out of this world! *Alien Superstar* has it all . . . action, suspense, and big laughs!"

—Jeff Kinney, author of the Diary of a Wimpy Kid series

"Henry Winkler and Lin Oliver keep us laughing while slipping in a lesson for kids—accept everyone as they are, even if they have suction cups for feet . . . A super fun read."

—Jennifer Garner

"Out of this world . . . will resonate with any kid who has felt like an outsider."

—*Booklist*

"A funny interstellar adventure that will have readers watching the cosmos for the second book to arrive."

—*School Library Journal*

LIGHTS, CAMERA, DANGER!

BY HENRY WINKLER AND LIN OLIVER

ILLUSTRATED BY ETHAN NICOLLE

Amulet Books

New York

To all the people who are there for us during this
pandemic and for Stacey, always!
—H.W.

For Theo, Oliver, and Cole . . . who grew from
our boys to fine men.
—L.O.

Cataloging-in-Publication Data has been applied for and may be obtained from the
Library of Congress.

ISBN 978-1-4197-4099-2

Amulet Books are available at special discounts when purchased in quantity for
premiums and promotions as well as fundraising or educational use. Special editions
can also be created to specification. For details, contact specialsales@abramsbooks.com
or the address below.

Amulet Books® is a registered trademark of Harry N. Abrams, Inc.

ABRAMS The Art of Books
195 Broadway, New York, NY 10007
abramsbooks.com

1

"**G**et your long, spiny fingers off my arm, you heartless ignorant automaton," Grandma Wrinkle snapped. She tried to pull herself free from her guard's viselike grip, but her strength was no match for his. Even though her spirit was strong, Grandma Wrinkle's physical strength at 987 years old was not what it had been when she was a young alien of 113.

"Save your breath, old turtle," the guard responded. He was at least seven feet tall with shoulders just as wide. "Where you're going, no one is going to be able to hear you, anyway."

The Squadron guards had been sent to Grandma Wrinkle's prison pod to bring her to the Supreme Commander, but she was refusing to go. Unlike all the other citizens on her planet, Grandma Wrinkle had the courage to resist government orders. She had no use for her planet's repressive regime, and she was not afraid to say so. Even after all those weeks alone in her prison pod, she remained unafraid.

Two male guards surrounded her, grabbing her by the arm while the one female guard held her by the scruff of her neck. Grandma Wrinkle planted her suction cup feet firmly on the metallic floor, hoping they would hold her in place, but she wasn't as young as she used to be, and so all it took was one shove from the powerful female guard to break the suction and send Grandma Wrinkle hurtling out of her pod and into the long, white hall.

"Where are you taking me?" Grandma Wrinkle asked. "As the former master mechanic of our spaceship fleet, I have the right to know."

"You don't work for this planet's government anymore," the female guard growled in her raspy voice. "You're our prisoner and you have no rights."

"I've done nothing wrong."

"You built a faster-than-light vehicle that your grandson, Citizen Short Nose, used to escape to Earth. The Supreme Commander has ordered that he be captured and returned to our planet immediately. He is a traitor and must be punished."

"You're all fools," Grandma Wrinkle said, "blindly

following a brutal government. My grandson was about to have his sensory enhancer neutralized. Deactivated. They were going to take away his ability to experience the joys of life—music, art, film, stories, beauty. I couldn't have him turned into a robot like you."

On hearing those words, one of the male guards, who was missing two of his six eyes, stopped walking. A faraway look came over his four good eyes, as if he were remembering some distant and pleasant memory. It was the sound of his mother's voice, soothing him to sleep in his baby pod. A warm feeling came over him, and he loosened his grip on Grandma Wrinkle's arm.

The female guard, whose name, Citizen Cruel, had been given to her for obvious reasons, noticed the softening of her coworker's face. She stared at him, her catlike eyes glowing golden with anger. Her gaze was so fierce that the guard had to hold his hand up to protect himself from her intense yellow glare.

"Citizen Four Eyes, do not listen to the words of this old woman," she commanded. "She will lead you down the path of forbidden memories. If you can't control your emotional weakness, I will disqualify you from entering the Body Snatcher Unit."

"Oh, please don't do that, Citizen Cruel," the four-eyed

guard begged. "I have been training to be a body snatcher my whole life, and my final assessment is very soon now."

"I'm on the selection panel, and I'll be watching you," Citizen Cruel said. "We Body Snatchers are an elite unit, and only the strongest and toughest are chosen."

"You mean, only the cruelest," Grandma Wrinkle said.

"No one asked you," Citizen Cruel barked. "Keep your two tongues silent or I'll tie them in a knot."

The group marched in silence down the long, white hall, past porthole windows that let in shafts of rust-colored light from the red dwarf sun outside. Grandma Wrinkle tried to look through the windows to see where she was. She caught brief glimpses of broken-down mechanical parts—fragments of interstellar fighters and busted-up afterburners. She realized that she was in the Cemetery, an earthen pit that was the final resting place of obsolete vehicles, a place she knew well. It was where she had built her grandson's escape vehicle.

"Eyes straight ahead, you mouthy pest," Citizen Cruel ordered. "All six of them. Unless you want me to poke out a couple, so you'll look like Four Eyes over there."

Grandma Wrinkle rotated all her eyeballs to the front of her head, and the group marched down the hall silently. The only sound was the echo of their suction cups bouncing off the floor. Soon, they reached a dead end. Citizen Cruel took a deep breath and blew onto the blank wall in front of her.

"I detect your breath, Citizen Cruel," a mechanical voice said. "You may enter."

"Walk, turtle," Citizen Cruel ordered, giving Grandma Wrinkle a hard shove.

"Into the wall?" Grandma Wrinkle answered. "That's stupid. But that's what you people do . . . follow orders even if they make no sense."

Citizen Cruel glared at Grandma Wrinkle, her yellow cat eyes squinting in anger. She grabbed Grandma Wrinkle and pushed. Just before the old woman slammed into the wall, it slid open, revealing a shining blue chasm.

"Get in," Citizen Cruel commanded.

"I've heard about this elevator." Grandma Wrinkle showed no fear as she spoke, only defiance. "It has one destination—the Cavern of Questions. It's useless to take me there. You'll get no information from me."

"Oh, I'm not worried. We have our special ways to persuade you to talk."

"You mean torture," Grandma Wrinkle said.

"Some people might call it that. We prefer to call it heightened persuasion."

Citizen Cruel laughed. It was an ugly sound, like someone choking on a chicken bone.

"Perhaps Citizen Bulk can demonstrate his heightened powers of persuasion now," she wheezed.

Citizen Bulk pointed one of his seven fingers at Grandma Wrinkle and an electric current shot out, making a crackling sound. The old woman shuddered as the current ran down her spine and she tumbled into the elevator headfirst. She couldn't speak, but if she could have, she would have said words that would get the average Earth kid grounded for at least six months.

The elevator shot down with such a strong g-force that everybody's cheeks jiggled. The four-eyed guard turned a little green and grabbed his stomach.

"I may toss my nutritional wafers," he said.

"If you want to qualify for the Body Snatcher Corps, you better toughen up right now," Citizen Cruel warned. "If you can't even hold your wafers down, what good are you?"

The elevator plummeted deep down into the core of the planet, breaking through a crusty mantle and entering a liquid ocean that glowed red-hot. As they traveled deeper and deeper toward the planetary core, the red-hot glow turned to yellow-hot then finally to white-hot, making the temperature in the elevator shoot up to an almost unbearable degree. Everyone, from Grandma Wrinkle to all three guards, began to sweat from their cobalt-blue skin.

Just when the heat inside seemed no longer tolerable, the elevator came to a screeching halt. The wall slid open, and there he was, the Supreme Leader, standing on a floating platform in the center of the Cavern of Questions. He was in his full military uniform, with laser swords hanging from his shiny spacesuit.

"What took you so long?" he shouted across the giant hall. "You were supposed to have her here seven minutes ago."

"She's a talker, sir," Citizen Cruel said. "She tried to resist.

We had to use Citizen Bulk's laser finger to subdue her."

"Stand her up and drag her to me," the Supreme Leader ordered. He was not someone who tolerated excuses.

With Citizen Cruel on one side and Citizen Bulk on the other, Grandma Wrinkle was brought before him. From his floating platform, the Supreme Leader looked down on her with his row of cold, hateful eyes.

"Look at me," he ordered.

Grandma Wrinkle did not look up.

"I think the heat has overwhelmed her," Citizen Four Eyes said. "After all, she is very old and her body is frail. My grandmother was frail too."

"Citizen Four Eyes seems to have a soft spot for this traitor," Citizen Cruel said. "He is showing signs of weakness. I have warned him that compassion is unacceptable."

The Supreme Leader stepped off his platform and floated down to the ground.

"I am not unkind, as many say," he said to Citizen Four Eyes. "And to prove that, I will not have you banished. Instead, you are to be taken to the reeducation unit until I am assured that this small-minded emotional behavior has been drummed out of you."

"But, sir, he is about to be tested for the Body Snatching Corps," Citizen Cruel said.

"That's out of the question. I will reexamine my decision after his reeducation is complete."

"Th-th-thank you for this opportunity, sir," Citizen Four Eyes stammered.

"Oh, shut up," the Supreme Leader snapped. "Your courtesy makes me cringe."

Citizen Four Eyes bowed and backed away, but he was so terrified that his weak stomach gave out, and he tossed his wafers onto the floor near the elevators. The Supreme Leader did not see this infraction, since he had already turned his full attention to Grandma Wrinkle. She stood facing him, motionless.

"Speak to me," he said. "We've known each other too long for this silence."

"I no longer know you, Citizen Clumsy."

"No one is allowed to call me by my childhood name. I am the Supreme Leader now."

"And your power has made you evil."

The Supreme Leader winced at her words. "Douse her with frigid air," he commanded.

"My pleasure." Citizen Cruel grinned. "She's a stubborn old thing who showed no respect for my authority, and I can't wait to teach her a lesson."

They put Grandma Wrinkle in a titanium chair, strapped

her in, and lowered a glass cage over her. Citizen Cruel went to a control panel and flipped one of the hundreds of switches, and a burst of freezing air shot into the cage. Within seconds, the glass became obscured with frost, and Grandma Wrinkle was no longer visible. A minute later, when the glass cage was raised, Grandma Wrinkle was shivering, and her cobalt fingers had turned an even deeper shade of blue.

"You know why we have brought you here," the Supreme Leader said. "You helped your grandson escape. No one leaves this planet without my permission. We cannot allow that. Do you understand?"

"Of course, I understand," Grandma Wrinkle said. "It's not brain science. You're a bully and you want everyone to do as you say. But some of us remember the way it was before you made yourself the Supreme Leader, when we were free. When there was joy and music and art and life here. I have sent my grandson off to Earth to experience such a world."

"Earth is a silly little blue planet where people eat pies made with tomatoes and cheese."

"It's called pizza," Grandma Wrinkle said. "And I hear it's delicious."

"Earthlings are empty-headed. I hear they wiggle their bottom halves to the sound of beating drums."

"That's called dancing," Grandma Wrinkle said. "They say it's fun. A word you have forgotten the meaning of."

"Earth is a trivial place. We will find your grandson there and bring him home. Once we deactivate his sensory enhancer, he will never experience joy again."

"You won't find him," Grandma Wrinkle said. "There are over seven billion people on Earth. And I have given him a secret identity. He looks just like any other earthling."

The Supreme Leader rose to his feet, and he used the voice activator attached to his neck to fill the room with sound.

"You will tell us where he is," he roared.

"I will not," Grandma Wrinkle said.

"I command you!" His voice rose to an ear-splitting level. The small bones inside Grandma Wrinkle's inner ear vibrated so hard they snapped in two.

"Never!" she shouted back, clutching her ears from the searing pain.

"All you have to do is answer one simple question," the Supreme Leader roared. "Where on Earth is your grandson, Citizen Short Nose?"

Grandma Wrinkle made the sign of the zipper, as if she were zipping her lips closed forever. She had seen Earth children do that in the movies she secretly watched with her grandson in the cave beneath her house.

"You leave me no choice," the Supreme Leader said, "but to turn you over to Citizen Cruel. She will get the information out of you. Citizen Cruel, are you up for the task?"

"Yes. But it will require physical endurance because she'll be a tough one to crack."

"Go to the Power Pole," he commanded. "I will administer a Super Strength Blast."

Citizen Cruel walked to a thick metal pole that was connected to a power generator.

"Hold the pole," the Supreme Leader ordered. "Citizen Bulk, flip the switch."

A buzzing sound reverberated around the giant room. Citizen Cruel's body became transparent, and all her organs were visible.

"That's enough," the Supreme Leader said. "Citizen Bulk, disengage the power!"

The buzzing sound stopped and Citizen Cruel let go of the pole. Her body came back to normal and her red lips spread into a wicked smile.

"I feel like I could fly without a vehicle," she said. "Super strong, super powerful, super mean."

"That's why I invented the Power Pole," the Supreme Leader said. "Go forth and do your work."

He jumped back onto his platform and floated high into the air until he was just a spot at the top of the cavern.

"Find that traitor," he shouted to Citizen Cruel, as he disappeared into the ceiling. "Use any means necessary."

Citizen Cruel looked at Grandma Wrinkle, and a crooked smile crossed her lips.

"We will get the information out of you," she said. "Citizen Bulk, bring me the Truth Serum, the one in the green vial."

"But we've never used that before."

"Exactly." Citizen Cruel smiled her wicked smile, her golden eyes aflame. "This is my date with destiny."

Then, rubbing her hands together in anticipation of the pain she was about to cause, Citizen Cruel laughed so hard that the sound of chicken-bone chok-ing filled the vast hall all the way up to the rafters.

2

It was a terrible dream. Even in my sleep, I could feel myself shivering from head to toe, like I had icicles in my veins instead of the thick purple blood of the citizens of my planet. The worst part was the horrible coughing sound echoing in my head, or maybe gagging was a better word, as if someone were choking on a chicken bone. That raspy, terrifying cough sounded heartless and inhuman. I wanted desperately for that dream to end, but I couldn't shake myself awake.

I heard a pounding on the door of my dressing room, but it sounded like it was a million miles away, coming at me through a thick, gooey haze.

"Buddy, they need us on the set!" Through the haze, I could hear my costar, Cassidy Cambridge, calling me.

I tried to answer her, but my mouth wasn't working. It was sound asleep too.

"Buddy!" she called again. "What's going on in there?"

I tried to open my eyes and respond, but they were heavy with sleep. Since arriving on Earth three weeks before, I was finding that I had to take naps every afternoon in order to stay awake. Maybe I was still getting used to the Earth's environment, especially in Hollywood, where the weather is hot and dry. There was no way even my expandable stomach could hold all the water I needed to keep myself hydrated, so I had to submerge myself in a bathtub at least an hour a day to keep my life force vital and my scaly skin from peeling off.

Sorry if the topic of my scaly skin grosses you out, but trust me, seeing me with scaly skin is a lot better than seeing me without it. Underneath, my veins look like wiggly, slimy worms expanding and contracting all over my body.

Ick. Now even I'm grossed out.

"Buddy, I'm coming in," Cassidy called, opening the door to my dressing room.

I sat up and shivered.

"It's hot in here," Cassidy said. "Why are you shivering?"

"I was having a terrible dream that seemed all too real," I answered. "I felt like I was tied up in a chair and someone blasted me with frigid air. And that a creature near me was choking on a chicken bone."

"Whoa, Buddy," Cassidy said. "Your imagination has

officially gone wild. Do you think you can check it at the
door so we can go to rehearsal?"

"It just felt so real, Cassidy. And here's the weird part. I
thought I heard my grandmother's voice calling to me."

"Buddy, your grandmother is twenty million light-years
away on a red dwarf planet. Even if she did scream your
name, you wouldn't hear it until you're old and bald."

"Hey, don't knock baldies," I snapped. "Remember, underneath this head of gorgeous human hair, the real me is hairless."

Cassidy laughed. "I forget that you're actually bald as an
eagle."

Since we don't have eagles on my planet, I wanted to know what I was being compared to, so I had my brain run a search of all the preprogrammed information it contains. I can process tons of obscure information in nanoseconds. It's just a thing we aliens do. Thousands of bald eagle facts poured into my head, and just for fun, I picked one to share with Cassidy.

"Did you know that bald eagles can see forward and sideways at the same time?" I said, standing up from the couch that had just been moved to my dressing room. (Not to brag, but I'd been told that having your own dressing room couch is the sign of a rising star.)

"Yeah," said Cassidy. "Their vision comes in handy for catching rats and other vermin."

"With my six eyes, I'd be really good at that too. My alien body is pretty cool, huh?"

"Speaking of your alien body," Cassidy said, pointing to my feet. "Your suction cups are showing."

I glanced down to check myself out. I was in my humanoid form, which looked exactly like Zane Tracy, a teen idol earthling whose movies Grandma Wrinkle and I watched in secret in her underground cave. Well, at least ninety-six percent of me was Zane Tracy. The toes on my left foot had started to recede and my real body's suction cups had popped out. The energy I use for my biological alteration must have been running low, and I obviously needed to recharge it.

I grabbed the titanium amulet I wear around my neck, the one that Grandma Wrinkle had made for me before I left my home planet. Clutching it in my palm, I closed my eyes and concentrated.

"Be Zane Tracy," I chanted under my breath. *"Be Zane now."*

But nothing happened to my suction cups. My toes remained alien despite my best chanting. And to make matters worse, my sensory enhancer, a trunklike appendage that grows out of the center of my back, shot up into the air and started to sniff my dressing room. Sensory enhancers love anything that you can taste, smell, feel, hear, or see. They have a mind of their own, which is why the repressive government on my home planet deactivates them when a citizen reaches the age of thirteen. Grandma Wrinkle, who taught me to love movies and art and music in her subterranean secret cave,

planned for me to escape to Earth on my thirteenth birthday. We both knew that enjoying the colors and sounds and feelings of art was crucial to happiness. That's why I was here on planet Earth.

But now, my mischievous sensory enhancer was acting up and making a beeline for Cassidy's hand. Instinctively, she pulled her hand away and put it in her jacket pocket, but it followed her, snorting and sniffing the entire way.

"Buddy, can you please call off your overactive appendage?" she said. "It's really annoying."

"Hey," I said to it. "Behave. What's got you all riled up?"

I know it's weird to talk to a body part, but the situation demanded it. My sensory enhancer ignored me, and just dove deeper into Cassidy's jacket pocket and snorted again.

"Wait a minute," Cassidy said. "I think I know the problem. I used strawberry-scented hand lotion this morning. It's got a pretty strong scent."

Cassidy took her hand out of her pocket and held it in front of the enhancer's snout. It inhaled deeply, then let out a loud noise that sounded like a cross between a fart and a moan.

"Is that an 'I like this' sound or an 'I hate this' sound?" Cassidy asked me.

"I'm not sure. Let me take a whiff too, and I can give you a better opinion."

I took hold of Cassidy's hand and put it up to my nose.

"Wow, that strawberry scent is strong. No wonder my sensory enhancer's in a snit."

"I'm going to go wash my hands in the makeup room," Cassidy said. "I hope the soap can get rid of the strawberry scent and the alien slobber at the same time."

"Excuse me," I said. "My sensory enhancer does not slobber. We don't have saliva on my planet."

"So you don't drool on your pillow when you sleep?"

"Never."

"Good to know," Cassidy said. As she left my dressing room, she called over her shoulder, "Hurry up and transform into alien Buddy. They're waiting for us on the set. You know how Duane gets if we're late. We don't want him to get his ponytail in a knot."

When I heard the door close, I sat down on the couch and got serious about transformation. Holding my amulet in my hand, I closed my eyes and chanted, this time putting all my concentration and energy into the words.

"*Be the real me,*" I chanted.

I closed my eyes and visualized the alien me. I could feel the titanium of the amulet start to heat up as the liquid crystal inside began to bubble.

"*Be the real me,*" I chanted over and over again. I opened

one eye and glanced down at my hand. It still had human fingers that smelled strongly of strawberry, but they were growing longer and looking more like my pointy alien digits.

Gradually, I felt an electrical current rising in my body. The hand holding the amulet grew so hot that my palm burned like I was holding a lit match. My forehead started to sweat.

"Biological alteration generates heat," Grandma Wrinkle always said.

I felt like I might black out when I was suddenly overcome by a melting feeling. I opened one eye and glanced at the full-length mirror on the back of my dressing room door. I could actually see my Zane Tracy face dissolving into thin air. I could feel the hair on my head receding into my skull and my familiar alien skin creeping up my neck and cheeks to cover my human face. My six eyes popped out and spun around my head. I noticed that they felt really itchy, so I reached up and gave them a rub, being careful not to poke them with my long fingernails. Within seconds, the itching grew worse, and I wondered what was going on. On my planet, the only thing that makes me itch is my allergy to the cleaning solution they put in our body vacuum cleaners. I have to use the solution made for babies, free of dried mycotic fungus.

I stood up and looked in the mirror, and to my shock,

I saw that each of my eyes had turned bright red, the same color as my lips. Then I heard a knock on my door.

"Hey, Buddy, it's Rosa from wardrobe. I was just coming to see if you needed any help getting into your costume."

I opened the door and walked into the hallway.

"Oh great," Rosa said. "I see you're already in costume. And hey, I like the new red eyeballs. Did you order new ones for this week's show?"

I could hear Rosa, but I couldn't see her. She was just a blur. What was happening to my eyes? I rubbed them again, and slowly I began to make out Rosa's shape.

"You okay, Buddy?" Rosa asked.

"Not really. My eyes are not acting like my eyes."

"Maybe those new red lenses aren't agreeing with you," Rosa said. "I'd take them out. I mean, they're cool but they're not worth suffering for. Just like high heels. I say get rid of them."

"I don't have high heels," I said. "My heels are just the normal height."

Rosa laughed. "You're a funny kid, Buddy. Now get going. They're ready for you on set."

As I walked down the hall, my vision slowly returned. I couldn't figure out what had caused my eyes to act up, but since it went away pretty quickly, I guessed it didn't matter that much. I decided to just keep an eye on it, so to speak.

Rosa walked next to me and gave me a friendly tap on the back. I noticed that she does that to everyone she likes, so it made me feel good. But my sensory enhancer didn't like it one bit. It flinched and let out a little squeak.

"Oh, did I hurt you?" Rosa asked.

"No, I always squeak before a rehearsal."

Just to make it seem real, I squeaked a couple more times.

"I know all you actors have superstitions before you perform," Rosa said. "Your costar Tyler has to wear the same red boxers every time we tape a show. And he won't let me wash them in between shows."

"Well there's something I wish I didn't know," I said.

We laughed together, and that felt great too.

"Buddy, you're so much fun," Rosa said. "We're all so glad you've joined the cast of *Oddball Academy*. I'm cheering for you every step of the way. Go get 'em, champ."

I turned and headed for the set, thinking about how much I loved these humans.

At least, that's what I was thinking until I ran smack into Tyler Stone. All it took was one scowl from him and everything changed.

3

Hey, creep," *Tyler Stone said.* "*You're looking* particularly freaky today."

"Thanks," I said. "I take that as a compliment."

"Well you shouldn't, because your fifth eyeball is hanging off your face and it's gross. Your socket is showing."

I reached up to check my eyeballs, and they were in place, all six of them in a neat row on my head. I realized that Tyler was taunting me. That guy would say anything to shake my confidence.

"Did you see last night's blue script changes?" Tyler said. "The writers gave me six more lines than you. They know who's the talented one."

It was my third week on *Oddball Academy*, and I was just now starting to understand the process of making a weekly television show. The cast starts out on the first day reading the script out loud around a table. The first script is always printed on white paper. Then while the cast works with the director to rehearse the show, the writers go into a room and do lots of rewriting. The rewritten pages come out on blue paper.

It was those blue pages that Tyler was gloating over, as he held them in his spray-tanned hands. He used to spray tan his face too, but Duane, our director, told him it made him look too orange on TV.

Jules, our stage manager, caught up with me as I tried to ignore Tyler and just walk past him.

"Buddy," he said. "Here are the new pages."

He handed me about fifteen blue sheets of paper. I held them up to the top of my head as I walked, which is how I read. People on my planet are speed-readers, and that comes in handy if you have to read every book ever written in the universe, which I did by the end of second grade. Tyler was right to brag. This new script was very Tyler-heavy. It wasn't going to take me long to memorize my part, since he had most of the lines.

I wondered what I had done to make my role so much smaller. In the last episode, I had a really big part. Ever since the audience had discovered me three weeks ago when I arrived on Earth, my part had grown every week. I didn't want to be fat-headed about it, but everyone was telling me

I was an overnight sensation. If that was true, why were they making my part smaller?

Was it that time during the taping when the suction cups on my feet got stuck to the rug and I pulled it completely off the set, couch and all? Or could it have been when I got a paper cut on my sixth finger and my purple blood gushed all over the prop pancakes in the cafeteria scene? The sight of my blood made Martha Cornfoot, our costar who was singing a song, screech a note so off key that it blew out her microphone.

I made a mental note to talk to Duane about exactly why my part had shrunk. Meanwhile, Tyler kept turning around just to smirk at me. I wanted to poke him right in his human belly button.

When we reached the set, Cassidy was already there, talking to our costar Ulysses Park. They were busy inserting the blue pages into the script and throwing out the old white pages.

"Ladies and gentlemen, boys and girls and children of all ages," Ulysses shouted in a voice that sounded like he had a vocal amplifier in his throat, just like the Squadron Commander on my planet. "Put your hands together and make some noise for the one, the only Buddy C. Berger! Heeere's Buuuuddddyyy!"

Then he made a bunch of noises that sounded like a huge crowd was cheering in his throat.

"Ulysses," I said. "What are you doing?"

"It's my impression of a talk show host, welcoming you to the set. You know, like Oprah Winfrey does. Or Ellen DeGeneres. Or Jimmy Fallon."

"I don't know any of those people," I said. "But they must be very enthusiastic. And loud."

Cassidy laughed, and as always, it made me feel good to

hear it. Her laugh sounds like the warm winds of Jupiter at dawn.

"Buddy," she said. "That's just another one of Ulysses's impressions. You know how he can make his voice sound like anyone or anything."

"Oh, now I get it," I said. "That was really funny, Ulysses."

"Way to miss a joke, doofus," Tyler said. "I could have traveled to Mars and back in the time it took you to catch on."

"Actually, your calculations are a little bit off," I explained. "It would take between seven and nine months to travel from Earth to Mars, depending of course, on the distance between the two planets in relationship to the sun. The average distance between Earth and Mars is 140 million miles."

"That's so interesting, I stopped listening when you opened your mouth," Tyler said. His thirst for interstellar knowledge was minimal.

Suddenly, a big voice burst onto the set in the body of Martha Cornfoot. Martha, who always said she was born to be in musicals, sang most of her lines in the script, and oddly enough, she also sang most of what she had to say in real life too. She told me just the other day that she'd rather sing than eat. Having tasted some of your Earth foods like lima beans and liver, I can understand that.

"*Hooray for Holl-y-wood,*" she belted. "*That screwy bally-hooey Holl-y-wood . . .*"

I had no idea what she was singing about, but she did it with such gusto I thought I'd better check. I ran the word *ballyhooey* through my Earth dictionary. The closest I came was the word *ballyhoo,* which meant *hoopla, hubble-bubble, hubbub,* or *hullabaloo.* Great, all that did was give me four more words I didn't know the meaning of. I was still nowhere, so instead I just said, "Nice to see you, Martha. And lots of hubble-bubble to you too."

"It's a big week for us," she said, linking her arm with Cassidy's. "Cass and I get to sing our first-ever duet on the show. I've been warming up my voice since seven forty-five this morning."

"What do you do?" I asked. "Tie a hot water bottle around your throat?"

"I haven't tried that," she said. "But I do everything else. Hot tea. Honey. Steam from the hot tea. Vocal exercises like Do Re Mi Fa Sol La Ti Do."

"I didn't know you spoke another language," I said. "I'm not familiar with that one. And I speak them all, except Hungarian. I have trouble with the vowels."

Martha looked perplexed. "It's not a language, Buddy. They're just sounds on the musical scale that help me free my throat."

"From what? Was it in prison?"

Cassidy laughed, grabbed my arm hard, and pulled me away.

"Buddy, you can't ask weird questions all the time," she warned. "People will suspect you're really an alien. And I don't think you want that. Let's keep that a secret between you and me and Luis."

"Speaking of Luis, have you talked to him today?"

"Yeah, he called me to say he's coming over after his shift to see how rehearsal went. He's excited about this week's show."

That sounded just like Luis. He was my first best friend on Earth, and he's stuck by me even after he learned I'm an alien. And let me tell you, that little fact freaked him out of his mind. The first time he saw me transform, he started breathing so hard he almost passed out. Since then he's gotten used to the idea and wishes he had suction cups for toes too.

I met Luis when my spaceship landed on the back lot of Universal Studios and he rescued me from the sight-seeing crowd. He's a stroller on the back lot, which means he wears a character costume, usually Frankenstein, and takes pictures with the tourists. He's only doing that until he gets his big break as an actor. I'm amazingly lucky because I got my big break on the first day I arrived here. That almost never happens to anybody.

"Poor Luis," Cassidy was saying. "He was in a really grumpy mood because they switched him from the Frankenstein costume to Woody Woodpecker. He says the beak pecks him from the inside, and he has to wear a Band-Aid on his nose."

"One day soon someone is going to discover how talented he is," I said. "And then he can say goodbye to beaks forever."

Suddenly, everyone on the set got quiet, which could mean only one thing. Our director, Duane, had arrived from his meeting with the camera team and was walking to the cafeteria set, carrying his script in a serious-looking leather binder.

"Good morning, everyone," he said. "We've got a lot to do today. We have nine new pages to put on their feet, so let's get down to business."

The first time I heard Duane say we were going to put the show on its feet, I thought the script was going to get up and run around the set and show us what to do. But now, three weeks into my acting career, I knew better. When you put a show on its feet, it means the actors stand up and act out their parts while they hold the script in their hands.

Yeah, I'm pretty much a Hollywood insider now. I know all the lingo. Like sugar glass. When you see a glass bottle shatter on TV, it's not real glass. It's sugar and water molded to look like a bottle. That's just one of the many showbiz secrets I know. You might say that when it comes to show business info, I know more than any alien you've ever met.

We started to rehearse. The first scene took place at lunchtime in the cafeteria, where we were discussing the talent show that the students of Oddball Academy were putting on for parents' weekend. The writers had made Tyler the host of the talent show, which is why he got so many new lines.

"Hello, parents and siblings, and welcome to our show," Tyler read. Then he looked at the imaginary audience, puffed up his chest, flexed his pecs, and flashed his toothy, white, movie-star smile for way too long.

"Take it down a notch," Duane told him. "You're playing the host of the talent show, not the star."

"When you have star quality, it just oozes out of you," Tyler said. "I can't help it. My muscles just flex themselves."

"We gave you this part because your manager said you needed more lines," Duane sighed. "But don't push it, or we can take them away and give them to Buddy."

"My audience wants to see more of me," Tyler said. "We both know that."

"Are you finished discussing you?" Duane said. "Because if you don't mind, I'd like to continue with the rehearsal."

"Actually, I do mind," Tyler said. "But carry on anyway."

"Okay, Ulysses!" Duane called out. "After Tyler welcomes the parents, you enter, stage left."

Ulysses was playing the first Oddball Academy student in the talent show, and the writers had him doing his impression of Joan of Arc. When Duane called "Action!" Ulysses came running in from the wings.

"Bonjour, everyone, which means hello, everyone," he said in a wild French accent. "I am Joan of Arc, zee most important woman in zee French history. I proudly give my life for la France."

"On May 30, 1431, Joan of Arc was burned at the stake for leading an army to defend her beloved France," Tyler read, wiggling his pecs again and flashing another of his over-the-top grins.

"Burned at the stake!?!" Ulysses blurted out. "Uh-oh. Change of plans. I do not like zee flames or zee fire or even zee smoke. Therefore, I am switching zee impression to Amelia Earhart."

Tyler cleared his throat and read his next line.

"In 1937, American aviator Amelia Earhart disappeared

when her plane went down somewhere over the Pacific Ocean," he read in an overly sad tone. Then he improvised the sound of crashing waves with a few seagulls thrown in, just to pad his part.

"Did you say plane crash?" Ulysses shrieked in a high-pitched voice. "I hate heights. I hate planes! I hate crashes! I don't even like to say the word *wings*."

Ulysses was so funny, the entire crew started to laugh out loud. The camera operators, the lighting people, Rosa the costumer, and even Lulu the boom operator were all cracking up, something they are not supposed to do. Even Duane *almost* smiled, which is rare. For a person who worked in comedy, he had no sense of humor.

Ulysses's scene didn't need much work, so they moved on to rehearse the next entry in the talent show, which was Martha and Cassidy's duet. While Duane worked with them to get that scene on its feet (sorry to use that show biz term again, but hey, that's what they call it), I sat down in the cafeteria set to give my suction cups a break. Sitting there in my very own chair with my name written on the back, it hit me that here I was in Hollywood, living my dream. Grandma Wrinkle had made this possible for me. I was overcome with how lucky I was to be there and how much she had sacrificed for me.

Suddenly I caught sight of something that seemed out of place. A large tree was moving from the back of the soundstage toward us. I rubbed my front four eyes, thinking that I was seeing things. I mean, trees don't walk on their own. Well, maybe they do on J407B, which is a deep space super-world planet with rings 200 times bigger than Saturn's. I hear strange things happen there. But on Earth, trees do not walk. They stay firmly planted just where they are.

Yet this tree, with its oddly glowing yellow leaves, was definitely moving at a rapid pace across Stage 42, and it was heading right toward me.

4

Cassidy," I said, jumping to my feet. "I have to tell you something."

"Not now. Can't you see Duane is working with us?"

"But this is really important."

I noticed that Duane, who had been working with Martha on the duet, had stopped talking and was staring at me with an expression that looked like he was sucking on lemons. It was definitely a sour look.

"Buddy," he said, "if you have something to say, why don't you just go ahead and share it with all of us. I mean, all we're doing is rehearsing a show that millions of people are going to watch."

"And they're very lucky," I said, "because you're doing a great job. And thank you for the opportunity to express my concern."

"Buddy, get to the point."

"Okay," I said. "The point is that we have a walking tree on the set."

Everyone turned around to stare at the tree, which was now completely still.

"Buddy," Cassidy whispered. "You're imagining things again."

"That tree was walking toward me just a minute ago," I claimed. "I saw it with all my eyes."

"Buddy, I asked the props department to bring us that tree," Duane said. "We're going to use it in the playground scene."

"But it was walking," I said. "Did you order a walking tree?"

"Let's move on," Duane said. "Buddy, you are interrupting our rehearsal time with nonsense, and I don't think your fellow cast members appreciate it."

"Yeah, my vocal cords were just getting into the warm zone," Martha said, "and now they're probably all frosty again."

"I keep telling you, this guy is a real amateur and is more trouble than he's worth," Tyler said.

"Buddy wants to apologize," Cassidy said. "Don't you, Buddy?"

"I'm sorry, everyone," I said. "I thought I saw what I saw but I guess I didn't see what I saw."

Cassidy and Martha went back to their positions on the cafeteria set, and I sat down at one of the tables.

"Your song in the talent show is about the joys of school lunch," Duane explained to them. "So put your heart into it. I want to taste and smell the fish sticks when you're singing about them. I want to feel the crunch."

"Obviously, you haven't tasted cafeteria fish sticks," Cassidy said. "They're definitely on the soggy side."

"You're an actor," Duane said. "It's your job to make the audience believe in what you're doing. Okay, girls, from the top. And . . . action!"

Martha and Cassidy started to sing. It was a really goofy song about how much fun it is to eat lunch at school.

Macaroni, crunchy fish sticks
Carrots, celery, cheese on toothpicks
Lunchtime's fun and all that food
Puts us in a drooling mood.

It was a catchy melody, and my seven fingernails were tapping out the rhythm on the table. Then my sensory enhancer started to get into the act too. It's very sensitive to music, and I could feel it start to sway in time to the beat. Duane noticed.

"I like that, Buddy," he said. "Good thinking to move your costume like that. I'll tell the writers to put that into the script."

Of course, I couldn't tell Duane that (a) it wasn't a costume and that (b) I had no control over it. When my sensory enhancer wants to sway, it sways. End of story.

I had almost forgotten about the moving tree, and just to reassure myself that it had all been in my imagination, I shot a glance over in its direction.

Wait a minute. Did I just see something sticking out from the leaves?

I slid a couple more of my eyeballs to the front of my face and stared really hard. There *was* something there, and it looked like a human face watching me. Looking closer, I could see it was a woman with a blond ponytail tied with a black ribbon. When our eyes met, a cold shiver ran down my spine. It felt like her eyes were scoping out my every move, just like a lion studies its prey before it's about to pounce.

"Excuse me," I blurted out. "I don't mean to interrupt again, but I have something urgent to say."

Martha and Cassidy stopped singing and shot me a look so crushing that if I were a boulder, I would have turned into pebbles.

"You don't interrupt actors when they're working on their scene," Martha groaned.

"I'm truly sorry to interrupt, but I promise you it's

different this time. There's a face in that tree that doesn't belong there."

"Buddy," Cassidy said, shaking her head. "This is not professional behavior. You have to get hold of your—"

Before she could finish her sentence, the woman with the ponytail jumped out from behind the tree. She had two cameras hanging from her neck, and she was holding a third camera with a long zoom lens.

"Over here, Buddy," she shouted. I could hear her camera clicking a mile a minute as she ran toward me. "Give me one of those alien smiles of yours. The fans are going to love those crazy red lips."

"I've never seen this person before," I said.

"She's one of the paparazzi," Cassidy explained. "They're photographers who sneak around taking pictures of celebrities without their permission."

By then, the photographer had reached the set, focusing her lens right on my face. She moved in very close to me and grabbed my arm, pulling me toward the exit.

"Hey, what are you doing?" I said.

"Taking you outside. I want to get a picture of you in daylight."

"No way," Duane said. "He's not going with you. We're in the middle of rehearsal."

"But I want to get a close-up of his two tongues," she said.

That was strange. How did she know I really do have two tongues? Everyone on my planet has two, and it is a work of genius. We can lick our lips and whistle at the same time. But how did this photographer know that? On Earth, I had always been careful to tuck my second tongue under the first one.

"Will somebody get security right now to escort our uninvited friend here off the set," Duane shouted. "She's manhandling my star."

The photographer just kept circling me with her camera clicking and her flash flickering in my eyes. She was taking close-ups of every part of me, from my suction cups to the bumps on my bald head. I thought I saw her catlike eyes emit a yellow glow, until I realized it was probably the flash from the camera making me see things.

"Stop that!" I shouted at her, but no matter how many times I repeated it, she wouldn't stop. She just laughed, a nasty, choking kind of laugh, and kept moving closer to me. I'm not sure what triggered it, whether it was the clicking of the cameras or something about this particular photographer, but suddenly my sensory enhancer leapt into action. It reached over my head, extending itself to its full length, and grabbed the camera, pulling it out of her hand.

"Hey," she yelled. "That thing's worth thousands of dollars."

But my sensory enhancer was out of control. It swung the camera around in the air, then tossed it into a nearby trash barrel.

"Nice shot," Ulysses called out. "You sank a three-pointer, Buddy."

"This is great stuff," Duane said. "Buddy, I love your costume more every day. Jules, get on the walkie-talkie and tell the writers to come to the set as soon as they can.

They've got to include this whole scene in the next draft of the script. And then call security to make sure the guards are on the way."

My sensory enhancer was on a roll. Swinging wildly in the air, it pulled me off my feet and dragged me over to the food line on the cafeteria set. Sticking the end of its trunk into one of the pots of prop vegetable soup, it inhaled the entire contents.

"Tell that thing to calm down, if you know what's good for you," the photographer yelled.

My sensory enhancer was on a mission to let this woman know who was boss. Pointing itself directly at the photographer, it let loose a torrent of vegetable soup right in her face. Potatoes, carrots, celery, and slimy bits of tomato splattered all

over her camera, her hands, her face, and her hair. A carrot slice even landed right in the middle of her black ponytail ribbon.

"This is hilarious!" Duane said. "We're doing this bit for sure!"

"You are going to answer for this attack," the woman snarled at me. "You'll see."

By then, two burly security guards had arrived on set.

"She's threatening my cast," Duane yelled to them. "Get her off the lot!"

"Not yet," Tyler said. "She hasn't even gotten a picture of me." Tyler struck his favorite pose. "Oh, and by the way, you'll want to shoot me from my left side," he said. "It's got that hunky little scar over my eyebrow."

"Tyler," Duane shouted. "Your timing is terrible. Besides, aren't there enough pictures of you in the universe?"

The two uniformed guards each took hold of one of the photographer's arms. She was really strong and tried to break free from their grasp, so they had no choice but to handcuff her.

"Get these things off me," she bellowed.

"Not until we see that you're safely off the lot," one guard said. "Let's go."

As they led her toward the stage door, Tyler called out, "By the way, did you get a shot of the scar?"

"Next time," she hollered back. She was talking to Tyler but staring at me with her creepy eyes. "I'll be back. You can count on that."

"Give me a little warning and I'll get my makeup done," Tyler said.

Surrounded by the two guards, she left the stage, keeping her gaze locked on me until the door slammed shut. I went and plopped down in my chair to let my enhancer calm down. There was something about the photographer that had totally set it off.

"Let's just relax, shall we?" I whispered. "She's gone now."

It snorted in anger and let out a noise that sounded like harrumph. I had never heard it say that before.

While I sat recovering, the writers arrived at the set, and Duane explained what he wanted them to include in the new scene.

"Okay, kids," Jules said to us. "Let's use this time for you to bank some school hours. Janice is in the classroom, and I'll tell her you're on the way."

"I'm out of here," Tyler said. "I'll be lifting weights in my dressing room. When you have looks like mine, you don't need school."

"Your brain is a muscle too," Ulysses said. "And yours could use a little workout."

Tyler just shot him a dark look and left. As the rest of us headed to the classroom at the back of the stage, I started to feel dried out, like my tongues were made of cotton. Usually I soak in the bathtub for at least two hours before I leave for the studio, but that morning I had overslept and had to cut my bath short.

Cassidy noticed that I was having trouble speaking because my mouth was so dry.

"You okay, Buddy?" she asked.

"I need to stop at Mary's snack table and get something to drink," I answered. "Maybe some avocado too."

Weeks before, when Cassidy and I had discovered that the ingredients in avocado were crucial to my survival on Earth, we had asked Mary to make sure that she always had lots of avocados available for me. She runs the craft service area, which provides all our snacks and meals during filming.

"Why don't you guys go on to class," Cassidy suggested to Martha and Ulysses. "Buddy and I will be right there."

When we were alone, Cassidy looked at me closely. In the three weeks we had been together, she had learned to spot the signs that my life force was dwindling and needed a boost.

"What do you need?" she asked.

"First I need water. And plenty of it. My sensory enhancer's reaction to that photographer took a lot out of me."

We walked over to the craft service area, which was at the back of the soundstage. When we reached the table, Cassidy picked up a pitcher of water and poured me a glass. I drank it down in one gulp, then grabbed the pitcher from her hand and guzzled that down. There were two other pitchers on the table, and I polished those off too.

"Looks like somebody's worked up a powerful thirst," Mary said.

"Can I have two more pitchers, please?" I asked her, my mouth still dry as the Draco Desert on my home planet.

"Sure can, honey. I hope that costume comes off easy because somebody's going to need to pee real soon."

"Do you have some avocados for him too?" Cassidy asked as Mary filled more pitchers with water.

"I had bought Buddy a few nice soft ones," Mary said, "but I just gave them away to Tyler. He said you told him you didn't want any today."

"I never had that conversation with him," I said. "He took them because he knew I wanted them."

"Oh, that's Tyler for you," Mary said. "I think maybe he's jealous of you."

"I'm not trying to make him jealous."

"Yeah, and that makes him even more jealous! My advice is to be the bigger person. He's in his dressing room. I bet if you go ask him, he'll share those avocados with you."

Yeah, right. The odds of Tyler sharing anything with me were a million billion trillion to one.

"I'll call Luis and ask him to bring over some of his grandmother's guacamole when his shift is finished," Cassidy told me. "He's coming by after work anyway."

"Here," Mary said, handing me a bowl of bright-red fruit. "Munch on some strawberries instead. I just picked these beauties up this morning at the farmers' market."

"I've seen those fruits before but never tasted them."

"You're missing out, Buddy. A ripe, juicy strawberry is like a little piece of heaven on Earth."

I took one of the strawberries and popped the whole thing into my mouth. The sweet flavor tasted delicious, but my sensory enhancer had another opinion. Immediately, it started to shake like it was shivering from the cold. Then the roof of my mouth began to itch. I scratched it with my upper tongue, but the more I rubbed, the more it itched, so I got my lower tongue involved too. It was a lot of mouth action.

"Honey, what are you doing?" Mary asked. "Whatever it is, you need to stop. That is not an attractive look."

I could feel Cassidy's hand on my shoulder. "Buddy," she said. "Your eyes are turning bright red."

"Maybe he has a strawberry allergy," Mary suggested. "My best friend, Olivia, has one, and it makes her break out in a red rash in that little space right under her nose."

"It threally thitches," I muttered.

Mary looked at Cassidy. "Do you have any idea what he just said, because I sure don't."

"I think he's saying it really itches. Maybe I'll take him to the set doctor to get something to calm that down. Come on, Buddy."

As I turned away from the table and followed Cassidy, I bumped smack into a light stand. I hadn't even seen it there. I realized that I couldn't see anything in front of me. It was all a blur.

"It's happening again," I said to Cassidy, my heart pounding with sudden fear.

"What is?"

"I can't see. It happened earlier this morning too."

"But it went away, right? Let's just try to stay calm and wait here a minute."

Cassidy helped me sit down on one of the folding chairs, and we waited. It took a few minutes, but soon my vision started to clear up. I began to see some images—first the craft service area, then the light stands that were surrounding me, and finally the overhead pipes holding the lights that illuminate the set.

"Can you see now?" Cassidy asked.

"Better. And I think I figured out what happened to me. It was an allergic reaction."

"How can you be sure?"

"Because it happened this morning too, when I touched your hand."

"Oh, great. So now you're allergic to me?"

"No, you were wearing strawberry-scented lotion, remember?"

"Ohhhhh . . . so it really is the strawberries. I guess I won't be baking you a strawberry shortcake for your birthday."

Cassidy stood up and helped me to my feet.

"My eyes are better now," I said, "but the rest of me isn't so great. I could use a long soak and a mountain of guacamole."

I could hear our teacher, Janice, calling us to the classroom. We had at least an hour of class, and after that, a full rehearsal. Somehow, I was going to have to power through the afternoon, but from the way my head was throbbing, the chances of that were not looking good.

5

Our classroom is a little room in the corner of Stage 42, which also serves as a prop storage area. Being right there on the stage makes it easy for us to put in our mandatory four hours of school a day. It doesn't look like any classroom I'd ever seen in the Earth movies I'd watched with Grandma Wrinkle. There are no bulletin boards or teacher's desk—just a round table with five chairs and a globe in the center. All the shelves are filled with weird props that we've used on the show. There's a stuffed crow, a banjo, a foosball game, a rack of wigs from every period in history, a shelf of false teeth, a fake space vehicle built on top of a two-wheeler bike, plastic hatchets and shields, and lots of pretend cafeteria food.

Our teacher, Janice, believes in letting us learn at our own pace and in our own style. We don't take tests; we just experience learning. When we studied ancient Rome,

Ulysses developed his impression of Julius Caesar that was a cross between Darth Vader and Homer Simpson. Tyler took a wedge of gray clay and sculpted himself as a Roman god throwing a lightning bolt. Cassidy learned to play the cithara (which is a small Roman harp) and played backup for a rap song that Martha wrote called, "I Came, I Saw, I Conquered." As for me, I learned Latin and memorized all the speeches of Mark Anthony. Janice couldn't believe it took me only a few days to learn all that. I didn't tell her that it actually took me just forty-three seconds.

I walked slowly from the craft service area to the classroom and took a seat at the table.

"Today, I have a lesson prepared on static electricity," Janice said. "It's what happens when friction causes an imbalance between negative and positive charges in an object."

"Like when you rub a balloon on your head and it makes your hair stand straight up," Martha said.

"Or when your underpants cling to your jeans," Ulysses added. "That happens to me all the time. I'm always having to do that tugging thing to separate them."

"That's what we call TMI," Cassidy said.

"You mean thermo-macro-interactivity?" I asked. "I'd love to discuss that. It's always a fascinating subject."

"Buddy, TMI stands for too much information, like

you're giving now," Martha said. "And, Janice, no offense, but static electricity isn't exactly grabbing my interest."

"Okay, let's focus on something you'd like to learn about science," Janice said. "I'm open to suggestions."

"I want to know how that robotic thing on Buddy's back works," Ulysses said. "Is it remote controlled with servomotors and stuff, or is it old school, like with ropes and pulleys?"

I wasn't prepared to answer that. These were my friends and I hated to lie to them. But I certainly couldn't tell him the truth, that the sensory enhancer was as much a part of my body as my suction cups or my two tongues. That would definitely be too much TMI.

"This costume is a delicate piece of scientific work," I said, deliberately trying to be vague. "I've been working on it since I was a baby."

That wasn't a total lie. I had been working on my sensory enhancer since I was a baby, because it came with my body.

"I have an idea," Martha said. "Why don't you take it off and lay it on the table so we can open it up and see how it works."

"I'll get a scissor," Ulysses said.

"The scientific method is to experiment, explore, and record what you find," Janice said. "Go ahead and detach the moving appendage, Buddy, and we'll see how the robotics work."

"Uh, I can't do that, Janice."

"Why not?"

"My reasons are very personal, and I'd rather not go into them."

Martha's eyes lit up. "Oh, I get it," she said. "You really are an alien and that thing growing out of your back is part of your weird body."

"That's science fiction, Cornfoot," Ulysses said with a laugh. "Not real science."

I was very relieved that the conversation stopped when the stage door flew open and Delores Cambridge barged in. Delores is Cassidy's mother and manages both of our careers. She manages not only our careers but also every breath we take. She's what you earthlings call a control freak.

"Heeeeere's Delores," Ulysses said in his television announcer voice.

"Knock it off, Ulysses," Delores barked. "If you can't do new material, don't do any at all. Oh, and here's another star tip. Cut your hair. Take an inch off the top so it doesn't look like a rooster's sitting on your head."

Poor Ulysses slumped in his seat at the table. Delores has a way of sucking all the confidence out of you in just a few words.

"Buddy, Cassidy," Delores said, rattling a large shopping bag that was draped over her arm. "I need to see you right now."

"Excuse me, Delores," Janice said, "we have very limited classroom time and right now, we're in the middle of a science unit."

"Don't get me wrong, I'm all for science," Delores said, "but I have pressing show business matters to discuss.

Science has been around thousands of years—it can wait one more minute."

You don't argue with Delores, because even if you did, you'd lose. Cassidy and I followed her out the stage door. The sun felt blinding, and the sudden burst of heat reminded me that I was still weak. I swiveled all my eyes to the front and used my hands as a visor to shield them from the harsh light. That didn't help much, so I leaned up against a parked golf cart for support.

"I have great news," Delores began, bringing her sunglasses down from the top of her head to cover her eyes. The lenses were so big, they took up her entire face. She resembled the red dung beetles on my home planet, and that's not a compliment.

"We've heard from Nike, and they've invited you both to make a special guest appearance at their new flagship store's opening tonight." Delores announced this like she was announcing the arrival of the president of the United States. Obviously, this Nike person was someone very important.

I wasn't familiar with him, so I ran the name through my Earth English dictionary. Within a nanosecond, it told me that Nike was the Greek goddess of victory. She had wings and everything.

"Whoa," I said to Delores. "I didn't know you actually

spoke to goddesses. How did the goddess Nike get in touch with you? Did the message come on a lightning bolt? Or did you hear it in a clap of thunder?"

Delores raised her sunglasses and looked me right in all six eyes, which is not easy to do.

"Buddy, there's a time for jokes, and there's a time for not jokes. This is a not joke time. An offer to attend the Nike party is about the biggest thing that can happen to your career and you need to take it seriously."

"Mom, of course Buddy knows that Nike is only the biggest athletic shoe company in the world," Cassidy said, her eyes practically boring a hole in me. "Don't you know that, Buddy?"

"Oh," I answered, picking up on her tone. "Oh yes, of course I know that. I don't live on the other side of the moon, you know."

"Sometimes I wonder," Delores muttered.

"This is really exciting, Mom," Cassidy said, "but don't you remember that tonight is the night Martha and I are going to sing at the Open Mic night at the Silverlake Café. We're trying out the cafeteria song we're doing in the show this week."

"Remember? Of course I do, I booked it," Delores said. "But Nike is just a little more important than a local sing-along with twenty people in the audience."

"But, Mom, I promised Martha. I can't disappoint her."

"Okay, okay," Delores groaned. "I'll take you to the café right after the Nike party. If we go directly there, you'll make it in time."

"You think we can fit in both?" Cassidy asked.

"Sure, if you skip dinner. Which is not a bad thing . . . you could stand to cut down on some calories."

I glanced at Cassidy and saw the pained look on her face. Her mother never missed a chance to remind her about her weight. Delores didn't seem to notice Cassidy's hurt feelings.

When it came to other people, even her daughter, Delores didn't notice much.

"Here's the deal," Delores said. "In this bag I have two custom-made pair of Nike shoes, designed especially for you. All you guys have to do is come to the party at the Nike store and wear them. It's going to be filled with press and on-camera opportunities. Everyone who's anyone will be there, and the promotion team has invited you two to represent *Oddball Academy*."

"Is the rest of the cast coming too?" Cassidy asked.

"Nope. The shoe company just wants the two of you."

"Tyler's not going to like this," I said.

"Then don't mention it him," Delores advised. "What he doesn't know won't hurt him. This is a major publicity opportunity. And wait until you see these shoes Nike made especially for each of you."

"Cool," Cassidy said, reaching for the shopping bag in Delores's hand. "Can we see them now?"

"No, you can't. Hands off the merchandise. I need you to be surprised tonight on camera when you see them for the first time. Besides, I don't want you to get them dirty. Tonight you need to look perfect, like the stars you are."

"I don't feel like a star," Cassidy said. "Mostly I just feel normal."

"Star tip from me to you, my darling daughter," Delores said. "Don't ever let anyone know you feel that way. Take *normal* right out of your vocabulary. Normal has no place in show business."

Ulysses stuck his head out the stage door.

"Hey, you guys," he called. "The writers are back with a stack of new script pages. Duane wants us on set right now."

"I'll come pick you guys up at six o'clock exactly," Delores said.

I turned to go back onto the stage, when another wave of weakness washed over me.

"Delores," I said tentatively. "I'm not feeling really well. Maybe I should skip the party tonight."

"Oh, good idea." Sarcasm dripped from her voice. "And while you're at it, why don't you skip your whole career too. Here's my tip for you, Buddy Burger. The show must go on. Rain, shine, sick, well, in the mood, not in the mood. None of it matters. You show up. That's what stars do."

That didn't leave me a lot of wiggle room, but I tried anyway.

"How about if I come separately? I can catch a ride with Luis."

"Why would you do that?" Delores said. "We should all arrive together. It makes for a great photo opportunity."

"Mom, we need to get back to the set right now," Cassidy said, knowing that I really needed to get some of Grandma Lupe's guacamole in me to have enough strength for the Nike party. "Buddy and I can do the press photo together when he gets there."

"All right, have it your way," Delores said, pointing one of her shiny red fingernails right at my nose. "But I'm warning you, Buddy, you had better be on time. Fame waits for no one."

The unrelenting sun was scorching down on me, and I could practically hear my insides screaming for water. We turned and followed Ulysses back into the cavernous darkness of Stage 42. Cassidy could see that I was still unsteady and held my arm as we walked.

"Can you hang in there another hour until Luis arrives?" she whispered. "He said his shift is over at five."

"I'm not sure. I'm going to need to shove in that guacamole as soon as he comes."

"No offense, but your arm is feeling really dried out," Cassidy said with a worried look. "You better find a way to soak yourself in water for a while too, so you can rehydrate."

"How? There aren't exactly a lot of bathtubs at the studio," I pointed out. "I can't crumble up my body into a sink unless I shrink, and I don't have that ability."

"I thought you aliens have all kinds of superpowers."

"You've been reading too many comic books, Cass. I'm just your average alien."

"Trust me, Buddy, there is nothing average about you."

We went inside and Duane handed us the script changes from the writers.

"We've got a lot of work to do," he said. "This wasn't exactly a great time to disappear on me. Now let's get serious."

I had a whole lot of new lines and I had no idea where I was going to get the energy to handle all that.

"I hope that costume of yours holds up," Duane said, "because in this new scene, that thing on your back is going to be on extra duty."

"Did you just say *doody?*" I asked, "because if you did, you shouldn't have. Not in public, anyway."

"Buddy!" Cassidy whispered. "You can't say things like that on set. What's wrong with you?"

My mouth suddenly had no filter. Whatever was in my brain seemed to want to just fly out. Maybe my reduced brain energy had loosened my filter. That could be dangerous. I made a mental note of words I should not say, and *doody* was one of them.

I'm not going to write all the words here, but I'm pretty sure you can make your own list.

I put a serious expression on my face as we sat down at the table to read the new pages. I reached back and gave my sensory enhancer a poke to remind it that this was time to work. It didn't respond much, just let out a weak little whimper.

"That won't cut it, pal," I said, addressing both him and me. "You better wake up. We've got to give this our best shot. I don't want to get fired because of you."

This time, my sensory enhancer muttered something that sounded like the word *doody.*

That was definitely not a good sign.

What follows is the revised scene. You can judge for yourself if you think my sensory enhancer was up for the job.

6

<u>INT. CAFETERIA — DAY</u>

The Oddball Academy students are in the midst of performing the talent show for parents' weekend. BUDDY THE ALIEN is the host. He introduces ULYSSES.

BUDDY THE ALIEN

Welcome to our talent show, where Oddball Academy students compete to show off their unique skills. The winner receives a luxurious trip to Uranus, complete with a space-walking adventure and all the de-hydrated ice cream they can eat. It looks like cardboard and tastes like cardboard too! The first act is our master impressionist—make some noise for our very own Ulysses Park.

Ulysses comes out and takes center
stage.

ULYSSES

Ladies and gentlemen. I'd like to
present you with my impression of
Joan of Arc's horse.

He makes galloping noises by clapping
his hands on his thighs, then whinnies
in fear.

ULYSSES

Pardon me, mademoiselle. I must
stop here and leave you. I am not
fond of zee battlefield. You go
must get off me, and go into zee
battle alone, while I go back to
Paris and eat some stinky cheese.

Ulysses gallops off stage.

BUDDY THE ALIEN

Thank you, Ulysses, for a very unique
view of history, right from the horse's
mouth. And for our next contestants,
put your hands together for the
blended voices of Cassidy and Martha.

Cassidy and Martha come out dressed as carrots. The greens look like they're sprouting from their heads.

CASSIDY

We love it here at the Oddball Academy cafeteria.

MARTHA

We don't love the food, but we love the cafeteria.

Cassidy and Martha burst into their song.

CASSIDY AND MARTHA

Macaroni, crunchy fish sticks
Carrots, celery, cheese on
toothpicks
Put us . . .

They are suddenly interrupted by a noise coming from above the stage. They look up at the light grid to see Tyler, playing the photographer, suspended by a cable. He is wearing three cameras around his neck, and he's shooting pictures while being lowered toward the stage floor.

MARTHA

Oh no! The paparazzi have invaded
Oddball Academy.

(singing)

Help! We need somebody. Not just
anybody.

CASSIDY

Call security! Call the police!
Call my mom, she'll hit him with
her purse.

PHOTOGRAPHER

Look up here, girls. Yeah, that's
it. From this angle I can see right
up your noses.

BUDDY THE ALIEN

Get off our stage, you low-life
snoop.

PHOTOGRAPHER

I'll leave when I get the pictures
I want.

BUDDY THE ALIEN

No, you'll leave now.

PHOTOGRAPHER

Oh yeah, how are you going to make
me, you Martian creep.

BUDDY THE ALIEN

I'm from Uranus, and here's how we
do it on my planet.

Buddy the alien presses a button on his
chest and his costume suddenly goes into
action. The crazy arm on his back starts
to swing wildly, pulling him toward the
cafeteria food line. It sticks its trunk
into the desserts and sucks up a glob of
chocolate pudding with mounds of whipped
cream. Aiming directly at the photographer, it lets loose and blasts the chocolate pudding into his face.

PHOTOGRAPHER

I'm going to sue you for every penny
you're worth.

BUDDY THE ALIEN

Go right ahead. On my planet, we
use dried weevil dung for money.
Don't spend it all in one place.

PHOTOGRAPHER

You'll be sorry . . .

Buddy the alien's trunk reaches back
into the dessert section again and fills
up with lime Jell-O this time. Taking
aim, it catapults the Jell-O across the
stage, where it hits the photographer
right in his open mouth. He starts to
flail, which causes him to spin in fast
circles in the air.

PHOTOGRAPHER

Help! This is making me dizzy. I
mean, really dizzy. I think I'm
going to . . .

Lime Jell-O comes flying out of Tyler's
mouth, raining down on everyone in the
talent show.

BUDDY THE ALIEN

And with that, I think we should conclude our performance for the night. Thank you to the audience for coming, and if you got Jell-O-ed, there are wipes available at the door.

A security officer arrives, unhooks the photographer from the cable, and leads him offstage.

CUT TO:

7

By the time we finished reading the scene out loud at the table, the writers were literally holding their sides with laughter.

"I've got to hand to you, folks," Duane said, slapping Harrison, the head writer, on his back. "This scene is slapstick gold."

"I can't wait to see how the audience responds," Harrison said. "They'll be rolling in the aisles."

"That's never going to happen, because I am out of here," Tyler said, standing up from the table with such force that his chair tipped over backward.

To say he sounded angry is like saying that the North Pole is a little chilly. His eyes were blazing mad.

"What's the problem now?" Duane asked him.

"I am an actor," Tyler said, "and a star. I don't spin in circles from cables. I don't have Jell-O of any flavor spit in my face. And I certainly do not hurl green slime. I didn't sign up for this. I don't play the fool. That role is already taken by the outer-space dork sitting across from me."

"Lighten up, Tyler," Duane said. "We're doing a comedy here, and this scene is hilarious. Trust me, you're going to get huge laughs."

"Which I will be getting in my dressing room because that's where I'm going," he snapped. "You will be hearing from my management team."

Tossing the blue pages on the floor, Tyler stomped off toward his dressing room. The table was silent for a minute.

"I guess we could take the hurling down a notch," Harrison said.

"Not on your life," Duane answered, shaking his head so hard that his ponytail wiggled on his neck. "This scene is funny just the way it is. Tyler will adjust. Jules, give him ten minutes and then go to his dressing room and talk some sense into him. Buddy, let's you and me meet with the props department to make sure your costume is properly rigged to do all the stunts in the scene."

"Actually, Duane, I'm not really sure if my . . . um . . . costume is constructed to do all that," I said.

I was feeling worse by the minute, and my sensory

enhancer was getting weaker as well. It was needing avocado and water as much as I was, which makes sense because it's part of me. It's like if you're really hungry, your toes are hungry too, not just your stomach.

"Okay, let's take off your costume and see if we can give it a boost," Duane said. "Maybe add a little motor or put in more powerful batteries."

"It's not so easy to take off."

"Why . . . is it glued on?" Duane asked.

I was too weak to even continue the discussion. I looked desperately at Cassidy.

"Hey, Duane, why don't we break for the day," she said. "Buddy can fix his costume himself. We all know how he likes to tinker with it."

"Does that work for you, Buddy?" Duane asked.

"It works like *monkey poop*," I said. Uh-oh, my filter was totally unhinged.

"What did you say?" Duane frowned.

"He said it totally works for him," Cassidy answered. "*Monkey poop* is just Buddy slang for totally."

Cassidy helped me get to the soundstage door as quickly as I could. She pushed it open for me because I literally didn't have the strength to do it myself. When we stepped outside, we were once again blinded by the light. The California sun was still intense at five o'clock. My skin felt like it was on fire, and the heat from the asphalt burned into my suction cups.

"You look bad," Cassidy said.

"I feel bad. Bad as a bat with *diarrhea*."

"Buddy, you're talking like a two-year-old with a bad case of potty mouth."

"No, I'm not," I said. "I just feel like saying *eyeball juice* and *butt wipes* and *nose hair*."

"Okay, that does it," she said. "We're getting you out of here now."

"Fine with me, you *soggy diaper*."

Cassidy looked around and when she saw that no adults were nearby, she jumped into the golf cart that was parked outside Stage 42.

"Get in," she said. "We're going to find Luis. I'm not sure I can drive this, but I guess we'll find out."

She turned the key in the ignition. I crawled into the cart, curled up on the back seat, and we were off.

I can't say it was a smooth ride. I can say it was a wild ride. I can even say it was a dangerous swervy-curvy ride. We careened down the alleys between the massive soundstages, past the bungalows where the writers and producers work, up the hill to the back lot. By the time we got to the New York city street,

I couldn't even lift my head off the seat. Everything became a blur—the Moroccan village, the western cowboy town, the dinosaur water ride, the Harry Potter castle gates. It all felt like one of those roller-coaster rides I had seen in the movies.

Cassidy pulled up to the bungalow where Luis and the other back-lot characters change in and out of their costumes and go on lunch breaks. She honked the golf cart horn so urgently that some of the tourists spun around to look at us.

"Look, there's that alien from TV," a man wearing a

baseball cap called out. Everyone whipped out their phones to take a picture.

"Please guys, no photos," Cassidy said. "We are dealing with an emergency here. He's got an alien disease."

"Should we call a doctor?" the man in the hat said.

"Only if you know one from Uranus," Cassidy answered. She leaned on the horn again, and Luis came bounding out of the bungalow.

"Guacamole!" she yelled at him.

"I've got it right here," he said, holding up a pottery crock that was filled to the brim with his grandmother's guacamole. I reached out and snatched the crock from his hands and buried my face in the green mush.

"*Butt nose, reindeer poop pellets,*" I muttered, as I gulped down the avocado.

"What's with him?" Luis asked Cassidy.

"His brain filter is out of energy. He's saying the first thing that pops into his head."

"I hope this fixes it fast," Luis said.

Apparently, none of the tourists noticed anything wrong, because they were all standing around laughing.

"That alien's as funny in real life as he is on TV," said the man in the baseball cap. "Can we get a picture of that guacamole all over his face?"

Luis is really good at dealing with tourists, so he stepped right up to the crowd.

"I'm going to have to ask you to disperse," he said. "I see that the stunt show is about to start in five minutes. If you want to see a man on fire jumping out of a window . . . and who doesn't . . . I suggest you hurry."

That did it. The interest in my guacamole face immediately disappeared as they all hustled over to the stunt show area.

"How long has this been going on?" Luis asked Cassidy.

"He just bottomed out this afternoon," she said. "We had a paparazzi invasion and I think it depleted his energy."

I had licked every drop of guacamole out of the pottery crock with one of my tongues, and I was using my second tongue to clean off any remaining bits on my face.

"Water," I gasped.

"Are you thirsty?" Cassidy asked.

"I desperately need to submerge," I said. "My insides are as dry as the Phantom Desert on Draco 438."

"I've never been to Draco 438," Luis said, "but I think I get the picture. Let's get you into some water."

"We don't have time, Luis," Cassidy said. "We're booked to appear at the Nike opening in an hour. My mom will freak out if we're not there on time."

"Okay, you take the cart and go meet your mom. I'll get this dude to some water and meet you there."

"I can't walk," I groaned. "My suction cups are completely shriveled."

I felt terrible, but at least I was making sense again.

"I'll handle this," Luis said to Cassidy. "Now get going. We'll meet you at the Nike store. I'll be the good-looking guy with the spiky hair."

"And I'll be the wobbly alien saying *doody*," I said.

Cassidy sped off in the golf cart. Luis scooped me up and threw me over his shoulder, compressing my stomach against his collarbone in the process. That made me burp a cloud of guacamole fumes.

"Whoa, Buddy, we've got to get you some breath mints," Luis said. "Do not exhale again or I'll pass out."

"Just get me to water fast," I said. My head was clearing up from the nutrients in the avocado, but at the same time, my body was shutting down from lack of water.

"I know just the place," Luis said, breaking into a run, which jostled me even more. I had to struggle to keep my burps to myself.

With me flopping along on Luis's shoulder, we arrived at one of the biggest attractions at the Universal theme park— Jurassic World. It's a wild water ride with lifelike dinosaurs feeding in the tall grass by the edge of a lake. I know what you're thinking, that dinosaurs went extinct eons ago. But this is Hollywood, folks, where anything is possible, and animatronic dinosaurs still roam the San Fernando Valley. A huge brontosaurus stood drinking from the lake and I swear, he seemed to have his mechanical eyes on me.

"You're going in there for a soak," Luis said, lifting me over his head.

"Can we just talk about this for a nanosecond?" I asked.

Luis didn't answer, just tossed me into the air and hurled me toward the lake like a fast pitch at a baseball game.

"I guess nooooooooooooooot . . . ," I called out as I zoomed through the air. The brontosaurus cast a steady gaze at me as I hit the water hard.

And just like that, I sank to the bottom of Jurassic Lake.

8

There is one major advantage to having three lungs—you can hold your breath underwater for a really long time. That ability came in very handy as I drifted down to the bottom of the cold, green waters of Jurassic Lake.

Almost immediately, I could feel the healing effects as my skin absorbed the water, and I was hydrated inside and out. From my front eyes, I looked out at the thick, green vegetation that seemed to thrive under the lake. When I swam up to inspect it, I found to my surprise that the plants were made of plastic and secured with rope to the concrete bottom of the lake.

But like I said before, folks, this was Hollywood, the land of make-believe.

My body started to relax as I felt the water replenish my life force. My brain cleared completely, and I could almost see all the inappropriate words floating off into the water. I closed my eyes and let myself be swept along by the gentle current. Suddenly, I felt a surge in the current, as if the whole lake had been stirred by a giant spoon. All my eyes snapped open, and I saw a huge foot with three claws approaching me. That was followed by a second huge foot with another three claws. In case your math is shaky, that made two huge feet and six claws that were coming at me.

Before I could swim away, a large brontosaurus head with its mouth open splashed through the surface of the lake, heading for me. There was no doubt that the head belonged to those three-clawed feet. It picked me up, grabbed me in its teeth, and lifted me out of the water as if I were a feather. From the corner of my eyes, I could see Luis standing by the lake frantically waving his hands over his head.

"Help!" I yelled to him. "I'm being eaten!"

"Just go with it, dude," he hollered back. "Brontosaurus were plant eaters. Besides, he's not real!"

"Real enough that I'm in his mouth!"

The brontosaurus swung me wildly from side to side. I could feel the guacamole sloshing in my stomachs, which is not a good thing because guacamole is not supposed to slosh. Then with a sudden downward motion, the brontosaurus lowered me toward the water and split the surface with his gigantic head. I could hear his mechanical gears humming as he dunked me deep into the water and pulled me back up again. He was tossing me around so hard, I had no idea whether I was up or down. All I knew was that I had to get out of this thing's mouth. I wiggled like a fly in a spider's web, but I was clamped hard in the grip of its flat dino teeth.

A crowd had gathered by the side of the lake, and everyone was pointing and cheering.

"It's that alien from *Oddball Academy*," one tourist yelled.

"They've added him to the dinosaur show," a kid yelled. "This is super cool."

Easy for him to say, I thought. He wasn't about to barf while being swung back and forth like a wrecking ball. I could practically hear Delores's voice telling me that public barfing was not good for a star's image.

"You have to get out of there, Buddy!" Luis shouted.

No kidding. But how?

The mechanical dinosaur must have been programmed to roar on a regular schedule, because I heard a click from deep inside its long neck, like a timer going off. Then it opened its mouth so wide you could hear the jaws snap open, and out came a thunderous roar. I seized the opportunity and scrambled out of its open mouth. I ran across its tongue, leaping on the soft, spongy surface like it was a trampoline. Scrambling up a giant molar just in the nick of time before the mouth closed again, I hoisted myself into its huge nostril.

I had never been inside a brontosaurus nostril before, even a fake one, but it was a very comforting place to be. It gave me a foothold from which I could climb onto the flat surface of the dinosaur's face. I was doing just fine until one of my suction cups got stuck on a giant nose hair. I tugged hard and finally heard a loud pop as my suction cup released. It's a good thing that dinosaur wasn't real, because yanking on its nose hair would have been hugely painful.

I wasted no time scurrying out of the nostril and climbing up its forehead until I reached the top of its skull. From there, I looked out at the entire theme park and realized I was at least fifty feet in the air, with no way to get down unless I grew a pair of wings.

"I'm stuck," I called to Luis. "Send in a helicopter!"

"Slide," he called back, pointing to the dinosaur's long neck.

"That's a long way down!"

"You can do it, Buddy. Just hold on tight."

From where I was standing on the top of the brontosaurus's head, it was a very steep drop down to the bottom of its tail. I hesitated. Then I hesitated some more. In case you're wondering why, let me pause a second to confess something to you. Even though I have crisscrossed the entire universe in a faster-than-light vehicle, the truth is that I don't like heights. They make my heart race and I go all panicky.

"Buddy! Nike is waiting for you!" Luis yelled. "Just do it!"

"Just do it!" the crowd chanted. "Do it! Do it! Do it!"

I filled my three lungs with a deep breath, closed all my eyes but one (I kept the back one open so I could see I how far I had come), and sat down at the top of the dinosaur's neck. Letting out a mighty yelp of fear, I pushed off and slid straight down its bony neck at what felt like the speed of light. I must have slept through the science unit on dinosaurs back on my home planet, because unfortunately I had not remembered that the brontosaurus had spiney bumps all down its back. Sliding down those bumps made the ride extremely uncomfortable on the hindquarter part of my body that I believe you humans call your buttocks. I'm told it's also called a tush.

All the way down, I yelped in pain, counting the seconds until I reached the end of the dinosaur's tail and I could get back on solid ground. But no such luck. When I hit the end of the tail, it rose up and whipped me around with such force that I went sailing into the air again. I looked down and saw that I was heading for a raft filled with tourists below me. It was hovering at the edge of a waterfall and looked like it was preparing to go down. I remembered all the signs around the back lot for the Jurassic World water ride. It seemed like I was just about to go on it, like it or not.

I landed with a thump right on the lap of a beefy bald man with tattoos covering his thick neck. His bulky tattooed arms protruded from his black leather vest.

"I'm sorry to intrude," I said to him, trying to be polite.

He just stared at me, or at least I think he did, because I couldn't see his eyes behind his wraparound sunglasses. I thought he was either very angry or really, really angry, but I couldn't read his exact expression because his entire face was covered with dark-red facial hair. I couldn't tell where his mustache ended and his beard began.

"Hey," he said, in a gentle voice. "Can I have your autograph? I'm a fan. We oddballs have to stick together."

Well, that was a surprise.

"Maybe another time," I said, "when we're not about to go down the steepest water ride drop in the western hemisphere. Speaking of which, do you mind if I hold on to your vest?"

I grabbed on to his leather vest just as we crested the top of the waterfall and went plummeting down at an almost straight angle. The g-force was so strong, it felt like when I took off for Earth six weeks earlier in my faster-than-light vehicle. At that time, the g-force pushed my stomach flat against my back so that all of my bodily gasses were expelled in one thunderous burst. I hoped that wasn't going to happen again, because I certainly didn't want to fart on a stranger.

We careened down the waterfall, sending waves of mist flying in all directions. From my two left eyes, I could see Luis running alongside of the ride, getting soaked but never taking his eyes off me. I screamed all the way down, and my biker pal screamed even louder, raising his hands above his head as we sped down. People on my planet don't have hair in their armpits, and as I glanced up at his, I wondered if he combed it. There was almost enough there to braid it.

I was so relieved when we reached the bottom of the waterfall.

"Please exit to your left," the ride operator said as he docked our raft. When I climbed off, my legs were extremely wobbly, but this time, it wasn't from lack of avocado or water but from the adrenaline rush of the ride.

"Hey, what about that autograph you promised?" my pal with the hairy armpits asked.

He handed me a silver Sharpie from his pocket, and I signed my name on his leather vest, in a space right between the Incredible Hulk and Madonna. Then Luis and I took off running.

By the time we reached Luis's car in the employee parking lot, the air had dried me enough that I was only medium damp. As we drove down Ventura Boulevard to the Nike store, I used a beach towel Luis kept in his trunk to dry my back, being careful to dry my sensory enhancer really well. Trust me, you don't want to get a rash on your sensory enhancer.

Clusters of fans, photographers, and television cameras

were gathered outside the Nike store. When our car pulled up, all the fans screamed.

"Buddy, over here! Come shake my hand! Take a selfie with me! Sign my arm!" Everyone wanted a little piece of me.

A parking valet in a black bow tie came and opened the car door, and another one went to the driver's side to open the door for Luis.

"That's one sweet ride," the valet said to him.

"I call her Muriel," Luis said. "She's my best friend, aside from this little alien dude here."

"Hand me your key," the valet said. "I'll take care of Muriel for you."

"Man, do I love show business," Luis said, his grin as wide as the night sky. "What do you say we go party, Buddy? Sounds like they got some hot music inside."

I got out of the car and stood there, waiting for Luis to get the ticket from the valet and come around to meet me. But before he could get there, Delores suddenly appeared, her jewelry clanking and her high heels clicking.

"Well if it isn't Buddy," she snapped. "Nice of you to finally get here. Let's get you onto the red carpet right now. The photographers were just about to leave."

"In a second," I said. "Luis is just getting the ticket from the valet."

"He can't be in the photos," she said. "They only want you and Cassidy. He's a nobody."

"He's my friend."

"Fine, go be friends with him tomorrow. Tonight is all about you."

Luis had overheard what Delores said. I was too embarrassed to even make eye contact with him.

"Luis," I began to say. "I'm sorry . . ."

"Hey, don't worry about me," he said. "I'll just go inside and fill up on shrimp. You know, hang with the celebrities."

"No, you won't be doing that either," Delores said. "You're not on the VIP list."

"Buddy," Luis said, with a confused look on his face. "Tell them who I am. I'm your best friend. I busted the speed limit to get you here. You can call over the doorman and get me added to the list."

"Buddy," Delores said sharply. "It's now or never. There is no time to deal with this."

The photographers from the red carpet were shouting my name. I didn't know what to do. I looked from Delores to Luis. Once again, my eyes couldn't meet his gaze and I had no idea what to say.

"Hey, Buddy," a photographer shouted. "Can you get that

guy to move out of the picture. Come over here and stand on the X and flash us that alien smile."

I took a few steps forward and stood on the X. My eyes were blinded by the barrage of cameras flashing. I could barely see anything. But through the haze, I did see one thing. It was Luis, his head hung low, getting back into his car to leave.

9

nside, this was no regular shoe store. Quite the opposite. An ordinary Nike store had been transformed into the most elaborate nightclub ever, even bigger and wilder than anything I had seen in the movies I watched with Grandma Wrinkle. Colored lights were swirling in fantastic patterns all over the walls. Mirrors on the ceiling gave a top-down view of the crowded room filled with glittery people. A DJ was playing throbbing electronic dance music. Everyone who wasn't dancing was clustered around a long buffet filled with fabulous-looking finger foods, most of which involved gooey melted cheese.

When we first came in, I worried that my sensory enhancer would go nuts from all the stimulation, but it remained quiet. I think it was still recovering from the excitement of the wild water ride.

Without giving me even a second to adjust to the lights

and noise, Delores pulled me directly over to a man wearing a bow tie with stars and stripes like the American flag. He had a whole head full of hair that didn't seem to belong to him.

"That's Lyle Lizardo," she shouted in my ear. If she hadn't shouted, I would never have heard her above the din in the room. "He's the lead reporter for US AND THEM."

"For who and who?" I shouted back.

"US AND THEM. It's only the most popular magazine on every newsstand," she said. "Put on a smile and answer his questions."

She gave me a sharp nudge in the back, which definitely catapulted me into Mr. Lizardo's personal space.

"Nice to meet you," I said, extending my hand to him the way you humans do.

"Oh my, that's a lot of fingers you're wearing," he said, shaking my hand. "Excellent costume. Mind if I record our conversation?"

"He'd love it," Delores chimed in. A crumb from one of those gooey cheese appetizers flew out of her mouth.

Mr. Lizardo turned on a tiny digital recorder he was holding and lifted it to his mouth.

"Tell me, Buddy," he said into the device. "You burst onto the Hollywood scene like a rocket. You have fans all over the country, and *Oddball Academy* has a whole new life. What's the secret of your appeal?"

"I haven't tried to be a phenomenon," I said honestly. "Who I am just comes out of me naturally, like nectar from the honeywort plant on my native planet."

"Wow," Lyle said. "You really do stay in character. You've even imagined the flora and fauna on your made-up planet. That's the sign of a good actor."

"It's what I do," I said, trying to sound humble.

Suddenly, I felt my sensory enhancer start to stir. Was it the throbbing music or the spinning lights that woke it up? No, it was the half-eaten gooey cheese appetizer that Delores was holding. In one flash of movement, my sensory enhancer reached out and snatched the remaining bite from Delores's hand, inhaling it in one powerful snort.

"Hey, Buddy, give it back," she said. "I was enjoying that."

"Sorry, Delores, I couldn't help myself. It looked too delicious."

Lyle's eyes almost popped out of his head.

"That's an amazing costume," he said. "Tell my readers the secret of how it works."

"Oh, I can't do that," I said. "A magician would never tell you how he does his tricks. It would ruin the magic."

"And besides," Delores interjected. "The network doesn't

allow him to share show secrets. It's very hush-hush. Come on, Buddy. Let's go find Cassidy. And thanks, Lyle. Be sure you send me a copy of the magazine when it comes out."

With Delores leading the way, we crossed the floor to a makeshift stage where Cassidy was surrounded by reporters and fans.

"Hey, Buddy," Cassidy called out. "Get your alien butt up here. It's time to reveal our shoes."

When I got close to her, she whispered in my ear. "Are you better?"

"I'm fine now," I whispered back. "I'll tell you all about it later. It was very exciting."

"Hey, you two, stop the chatter," Delores said. "This is your moment. Seize it."

The flashing lights stopped and a spotlight shone on Cassidy and me as we took center stage. We sat on the two high stools, and a representative from Nike came out and presented us each with a shoe box. Cassidy opened hers first and pulled out a pair of silver-gray sneakers with her name in rhinestones.

"Wow," said Cassidy. "These are super cool. I can't believe you guys bejeweled my name on the sides. Buddy, what did you get?"

I opened my box and took out a pair of bright-orange

sneakers that were so wide an elephant could wear them. They looked like fluorescent flying saucers with shoelaces. Everybody in the room burst out laughing when they saw them. Cassidy and I did too.

"Look, Buddy, those will fit right over your suction cups," Cassidy said. "Let's try them on."

Cassidy put her shoes on first and everyone applauded when she walked around the stage like a model, showing them off at every angle. Then it was my turn. I slipped my shoes on, making sure my suction cups were all neatly tucked in before I tied the laces. Those sneakers were amazingly comfortable and made my suction cups feel like they

were resting on pillows. *It's too bad Nike doesn't have a shoe shop on my planet*, I thought. But then, the Squadron would never have allowed it. What the Squadron makes us wear is strictly regulated to be no fun. Everyone on the planet looks the same from the bottom of our feet to the top of our bumpy heads.

"Walk around and show them off," Cassidy whispered. "It's really fun."

As I stood up, the deejay put on some techno outer-space music, or at least, what you humans think outer-space music sounds like. On my planet, of course, music is forbidden because the Supreme Commander feels it sparks emotions that are hard to control. Controlling the population is his number one priority.

"Hey, Buddy, see if you can fly in those shoes," a girl from the crowd yelled out.

"Yeah, show us your moves," another person hollered.

True confession: I had never danced before, not even once, so I had no idea what to do. At first, I just stood there, thinking about how to move my feet. But I didn't have to think long. The music was so irresistible, my feet started to move on their own, slowly at first and then picking up speed to match the beat. I looked down at them and was shocked to see that they were twisting and twirling and pivoting and kicking high in the air. Before I could stop it, my left foot was over my head and wrapping itself around my neck.

Then my sensory enhancer got involved, and in a big way. Extending itself above my head, it started to swirl around so hard that it knocked me off my feet, and before I knew it, I was completely upside down, while it was spinning on the ground like a break dancer spins on his head. My shoes were up in the air, turning so fast that they actually looked like flying saucers.

Cassidy danced in a circle around me, clapping and cheering me on.

"Go, Buddy. Go, Buddy!" she chanted, and the crowd joined in with her. There wasn't a person in the room who didn't get caught up in the excite-ment. The entire crowd spontaneously jumped up and down in unison. It was like an explosion of energy and emotion.

If this is what being a Hollywood star feels like, I

thought, *count me in*. The only thing missing from this great moment was Grandma Wrinkle, watching me realize a dream I had held ever since we saw our first movie together.

When the dance ended, both my sensory enhancer and I were panting so I flopped down on the edge of the stage to catch my breath. That was a big mistake. I was immediately surrounded by a mob of fans, grabbing at me, trying to rip off any part of what they thought was my costume. A guy with spiky hair and an olive-green mesh tee shirt grabbed my sensory enhancer and yanked hard.

"Hey, let go of that," I said.

"Why should I?" he snarled.

"How's this for a reason."

With explosive force, my sensory enhancer blasted the remains of Delores's gooey cheese appetizer in his direction. I had thought that he might find that funny, but instead, his face turned beet red, and his eyes narrowed with anger.

"I don't like the way you're treating me." He scowled. "You owe me respect."

There was something in his eyes that was fierce, dangerous even.

"But I don't know you, sir," I said.

"Oh, trust me, you will in a second. I'm going to be unforgettable."

As he said those words, he leaned so close to me that I could smell his breath. It had a foul odor, like the rotten-egg stench of burning sulfur. I knew that smell from my planet. When volcanoes erupt in our planet's craters, everyone has to wear gas masks for weeks to block out the toxic stink of molten sulfur.

A wave of fear ran down my body. Who was this man with the terrible breath and why was he threatening me? I had been warned that some fans do not respect boundaries and a celebrity can feel threatened. He was definitely cutting into my comfort zone.

"Please don't make me have to call someone for help," I said to him. "You need to respect my boundaries."

"I don't care about your boundaries," he shot back. "Whether you know it or not, you're coming with me."

I thought I saw him reach out for my arm, but just then, a server pushed in between us carrying a tray with two large water bottles and a glass of ice.

"Your manager said to keep you well hydrated, Buddy," he said, "so she had us bring you this water."

"Hey, the alien and I are talking here," my aggressive fan said.

He reached out to shove the server away, knocking him off balance. The server stumbled backward. His tray wobbled and the water bottles tipped over, drenching my fan with icy cold water. He clenched his fists and let out a yowl of shock and surprise.

Delores heard the commotion and was at my side in a flash. She grabbed my hand to help me jump down from the stage.

"Leave him alone," she ordered the spikey-haired man, pushing him aside with her purse.

"I don't have to listen to you," he hollered.

"Oh yes you do, or I'll have you thrown out of here in a snap. As a matter of fact, I think I will have you thrown out. Someone get the bouncer to expel this clown."

In two seconds, a man with arms the size of thighs arrived and took hold of the man's tee shirt with a viselike grip.

"Go find another star to harass," Delores said, as the man was dragged away. "Oh, and while you're at it, you should get some mouthwash. Or suck on some industrial-strength mints. Your breath smells like a dead skunk."

Pulling on my arm, Delores cleared a path across the room, with her husky voice shouting, "Let us through," while she swatted at groping fans with her purse. She pulled me along like a rag doll, with me tripping over my new shoes until we reached a tall woman who was sitting at a round table on the other side of a red-velvet rope. I didn't know who she was, but she was clearly someone important. Next to her was a small man who was holding a phone to each ear. He seemed to be having two conversations at the same time, even though he had just one mouth. The woman stood up to greet us, and the small man put down the phones and unhooked the velvet rope to let us into the VIP area.

"Hello, Buddy," the tall woman said, holding out her hand. "I'm so happy to finally meet you."

"I'm happy to meet you too," I said. "By the way, who are you?"

"Oh, I'm Barbara Daniel. I'm the president of the television network that carries your show. And all of us are so thrilled that you have joined the cast of *Oddball Academy*."

"Yes, so thrilled," the small man chimed in.

He had slipped both phones into his jacket pocket and was now hovering around Ms. Daniel like a worker bee circling a queen bee.

"Buddy, we see you as a breakout star," Ms. Daniel went on, "and we want to promote you aggressively across the network."

"Yes." The small man nodded. "Very aggressively."

Ms. Daniel turned to him. "Chuck, I just said that."

"Yes, you did, boss," he said. "And it sounded a lot better coming from you."

"As Buddy's manager, Barbara," Delores interrupted, "I

can assure you that we're open to considering all your ideas. Although I do see him starring in his own series in the not-too-distant future. Don't you?"

"Let's take this one step at a time," Ms. Daniel said.

"That's a brilliant idea, boss," Chuck said. "One step followed by another step."

Ms. Daniel shot him an irritated look.

"Chuck," she said. "Can you go outside and tell the driver that we'll be another hour or so?"

"Sure, I'll call him right now." He reached into his pocket for one of his cell phones.

"I really think you should go outside and find him," Ms. Daniel said firmly. "The personal touch always works best."

"But wouldn't you rather I stay here and help you work out the details with Buddy?" he asked.

"It will be difficult to manage without you, but I've got this under control."

"As you always do," he said, throwing out one last annoying compliment before he slithered to the door.

"As a first step, we'd like Buddy to make a special guest appearance on *Dance America*," Ms. Daniel said to Delores. "It's in the most watched time slot of our Tuesday night lineup, and he can show the world some of those amazing moves we saw tonight."

"I'm listening," Delores said. "What else do you have in mind?"

"Game shows, talk shows, late night, you name it," Ms. Daniels said. "Let's discuss your wish list right now."

"Oh, I can't tonight," I said. "I promised Cassidy that I'd go watch her sing at the Silverlake Café."

"Buddy, can I have a word with you?" Delores said, pulling me away so suddenly that I tripped over my shoes again and almost did a face-plant right in front of the network president.

When we were out of earshot, she said, "Buddy, have you lost your mind?"

"No, I know exactly where it is. It's between my ears and behind my six eyes, where it always is."

"Once again, this is one of those no-joke times," she warned, wagging her red-tipped fingernail at me. She definitely had on her no-joke face. "Listen to me very carefully. One of the most powerful women in Hollywood just invited you to discuss your future, and you're going to say no because you want to watch Cassidy and Martha go sing some silly song? That's insanity. I won't let that happen. Yes is your only answer."

"But I promised Cassidy I'd be there. And besides, you're supposed to drive her to the café."

"Don't you worry your blue little self. I'll call her father and tell him to take her. You're talking to Delores here, and I have this under control."

"Won't Cassidy be mad that we're not there?"

"In a situation like this, she'll understand. Trust me, if the situation were reversed, she'd be having this discussion with Barbara Daniel so fast all of your fake eyes would spin in their sockets . . . that is, if they have sockets."

"Well," I hesitated, "it is a once-in-a-lifetime opportunity. And Ms. Daniel seems like a very nice woman. Maybe we can talk fast and I could still get to the café in time."

"Now you're using your head," Delores said. "Let's go make a deal."

We walked back to Ms. Daniel.

"I'd be happy to have this conversation now," I said.

"He means *we'd* be happy to have this conversation," Delores added.

"Great," Ms. Daniel said. "I took the liberty of ordering some guacamole and chips. I hear you're a big fan of the avocado. Now where should we start? A movie deal? A Super Bowl commercial? What's your dream?"

As I sat down at the table, my mind was swirling with visions of my show business future dancing in my head.

10

I'll tell you what happened, but please try not to judge me. The conversation went long, and I missed Cassidy's entire performance.

You are judging me—I can feel it. But let me explain.

Several times during the conversation, I attempted to remind Delores that I had promised Cassidy I'd be at the café in time to hear her sing, but each time I did, Delores brought up another topic with Ms. Daniel. Guest appearances on TV shows, my own YouTube channel, a cross-country tour, a TV special filmed at the National Air and Space Museum. I confess, it was all so exciting that I lost track of time. When we finally left the Nike store, it was eight o'clock. Cassidy's performance was at seven o'clock.

As we drove home, Delores was one happy camper.

"That was the best business meeting I've ever had," she

said as we drove down Ventura Boulevard and turned south into the hills toward home.

"I don't know," I said. "I think the guacamole was a little on the spicy side. Luis's grandmother's guacamole beats it by a mile."

"I'm not talking about the appetizers, Buddy," Delores said. "I'm talking about the conversation."

"Oh yeah, that part when Ms. Daniel told us she wanted to be an astronomer when she grew up was really interesting. She knew a lot more about space than most people in Hollywood."

"Space, schmace," Delores said. "Who cares? I'm referring to the conversation about building your career over the next five years. The future is nothing but up for us."

"For me and for Cassidy?"

"Right now, it's you they want."

"I feel so bad I missed Cassidy at the café tonight," I said. "I really hope she's not angry."

"I know my daughter," Delores said, as we pulled into the driveway. "She's a show business professional. She knows that whatever happens to you is good for the show. And if it's good for the show, it's good for her too. Of course she won't be angry. Come on, let's go in and tell her the good news."

As we walked up the front porch steps, Cassidy flung open the front door. I confess I'm not an expert at reading human emotions, but there was no mistaking this one. Cassidy's face was an open book that spelled F-U-R-I-O-U-S.

"Thanks a lot, friend," she yelled before I had even reached the porch. "Martha and I waited for you. We let two other acts go before us until we realized that you were not showing up."

"Cass, let me explain," I said.

"There is only one explanation, Buddy. You weren't there for me. Period. The end."

I turned to Delores, looking at her in desperation.

"Explain to her what happened," I begged.

"Cassidy, get over yourself," Delores sighed. "Buddy and I were having an important meeting."

"I know what's important to you, Mom, and it's not me or my feelings."

Cassidy turned to me, and I think I saw tears starting to form in the corners of her eyes. "Don't you understand, Buddy, I really needed you there. You promised."

"But the network head, she was offering me all kinds of amazing things."

"It was the first time I ever sang in front of an audience, Buddy, and I needed your support. Martha did too. You gave me your word. "

Cassidy spun around and stormed into the house. I tried to follow her, but she disappeared down the hall and slammed her bedroom door so hard the walls shook. Cassidy's little sister, Eloise, who was sitting at the kitchen table working on a Lego palace with her dad, had seen our whole argument.

"Somebody's in big, fat trouble," Eloise said. "Glad it's not me this time."

Delores threw her keys into a ceramic bowl on a table next to the front door and slung her purse over one of the kitchen chairs.

"I'm beat," she said. "I'm going for a soak in the bathtub." As she left, she added, "Don't worry, Buddy. Cassidy will get over it."

"Oh no she won't," Eloise said. "Yesterday, I borrowed her white furry cat pillow and by accident I got purple gummy bears all over it, and when I tried to wash them out, the hot water melted them and now they're stuck in the fur forever and ever. Cassidy's still not talking to me."

"Eloise, you know Snowball was always special to Cassidy," her dad explained. "You can't destroy your sister's property. That's why she was angry."

"But I didn't destroy anything," I said, defending myself. "I was just late and missed her performance. And I had a good reason . . . Delores said talking with the network president was an opportunity I couldn't pass up."

Mr. Cambridge stood up and reached for his jacket.

"You're not going yet, are you, Daddy?" Eloise said.

"Yes, honey. I have to go to my apartment because school nights you spend at your mom's house. I'll come back this weekend, and we'll finish our Lego palace. Maybe we can even start the heliport."

After Eloise gave her dad a big hug and they did their special handshake, which involved a lot of slapping of fingers and wiggling of hips, Mr. Cambridge turned to me.

"A word of advice, Buddy," he said. "Despite what Delores tells you, it's not always about opportunity. Friendship is based on trust and people keeping their word."

"That's exactly what your older daughter said."

"If I were you, I'd go have that talk with her," he said.

"Can I come and listen?" Eloise asked. "It's fun to watch people fight."

"You stay here and work on our palace," her dad said. "The drawbridge collapsed when your sister slammed the door. I'll see you before you know it."

That Mr. Cambridge is a really smart guy, but he's an architect and not in show business. He didn't understand that when your star is rising and you've got a shot at the brass ring, you have to grab it right away.

Eloise walked her father to his car, and I sat down at the kitchen table for a minute, to gather my thoughts for the conversation with Cassidy. I overheard a conversation going on outside, and I peeked out the door to see what was happening. There was a truck parked in the driveway, and Mr. Cambridge was talking to a man wearing a baseball cap and a uniform that said California Gas Company. He was holding a clipboard.

"As I just told you," Cassidy's dad was saying, "no one called anyone about a gas leak. Who told you to come here?"

"Orders from my commander," the uniformed man said.

"You have commanders in the gas company? That's strange."

"Oh, I mean my boss. My supervisor. My dispatcher. Whatever. This is 2416 Hollyridge, isn't it?"

"Yes it is, but you must have gotten the numbers mixed up. We didn't call the gas company."

"Maybe I should just come in and have a look around anyway," the man said.

"No, that won't be happening." Mr. Cambridge was firm. "You need to leave now."

"Sir, it's the law that I have to instruct all members of the household about our new procedures for emergency gas turnoff. Therefore, I must go inside."

"No, what you must do is leave the premises now. Eloise, go inside with Buddy."

"I don't like you," Eloise said to the man.

"Eloise, that's not nice," her father said.

"But he has mean eyes, like an evil wizard."

"She's only seven," Mr. Cambridge said to the inspector, "and her head is full of magic and spells and princes that turn into frogs."

I stepped outside and took Eloise's hand to take her back into the house. When the man from the gas company saw me, he didn't seem at all surprised. Usually, when people see me in my alien form, they either freak out or they recognize me from TV. He didn't do either.

"How long has the alien been living here?" he asked Mr. Cambridge, never taking his eyes off me. I had to agree with Eloise; there was something creepy in them.

"That's none of your business," Mr. Cambridge said. "And by the way, he's not an alien, he's an actor. There are no space aliens living on Earth."

"I hear there are," the man said.

He gave me a look as if that remark was supposed to mean something to me.

"Well, if you won't let me come in," he went on, "then I need to take you to my truck to go over the turn-off procedures. I'll begin with the alien-looking guy."

He reached out, took my arm, and started leading me to his truck in the driveway.

"Perhaps you didn't hear me," Mr. Cambridge said, stepping in front of me. "You have to come back during working hours, and if you're going to enter our house, I'll need confirmation from your supervisor."

"What are you, some kind of rule follower?" The inspector had a very aggressive tone, and Mr. Cambridge didn't like that one bit.

"Apparently I am," he said, taking out his cell phone. "I'm giving you to the count of five to get in your truck and leave, or I'm calling the police. One . . . two . . ."

"Don't get the police involved!" the inspector said, suddenly sounding alarmed.

"Three . . . four . . ."

"Okay, okay, I'm leaving."

Flashing me a nasty, crooked smile, the inspector tipped his hat and hurried to his truck. I noticed a glow from his eyes reflected in the driver's side window.

"What do you think that is?" I asked Cassidy's dad.

"Probably a reflection from his cell phone. He must be trying to call his boss before I do. I'm definitely going to report that guy."

"That's good, Daddy," Eloise said. "That man should get a bad report card just like Leo Gruntin in my class got for pulling on my braids."

The truck screeched as it disappeared down the driveway. Mr. Cambridge took Eloise's hand and we walked inside the house.

"That gassy man scared me," Eloise said.

"Nothing to be scared about," Mr. Cambridge reassured her. "I'll take care of him. Come on, I'll lock the door and make you some hot chocolate. I'll stay with you until your mom is finished with her bath."

While Eloise and her dad sipped hot chocolate with little white pillows on top (which you humans call marshmallows), I screwed up my courage and went down the hall to Cassidy's bedroom. I tapped lightly on the door because I was too nervous to actually knock.

"Go away, Buddy," Cassidy called out.

"But I want to talk this over."

"There is nothing to say, and I mean nada."

Nada. Even though it's in another language, I didn't have to search for that word in my Earth dictionary. I got the meaning loud and clear just from her tone of voice.

"Cassidy, I really wanted to be there for you tonight," I tried to explain. "I didn't mean to hurt your feelings, but you have to understand—this is a major career opportunity. Not just for me, but for both of us. I mean, it was a meeting with the head of the network."

There was a long silence, and I thought I had finally gotten through to her. Then the door opened, and she was standing in front of me.

I smiled. She definitely did not.

"Buddy," she said, her voice cracking with emotion. "Ever since I

met you, I've been there for you every step of the way. Taking care of you. Protecting your secret. Understanding your extreme weirdness. All I have ever asked of you was one thing—to come to the club tonight—and you didn't care enough to do it."

"But your mother said . . ."

"There are no excuses, Buddy. The truth is I really don't know who you are anymore. When you first came here, you knew nothing about show business, and now you put a meeting with a network executive first, before our friendship. I think we need a break."

"What do you want to break? Some dishes? A vase your mother doesn't use much? That should release some tension."

"No, Buddy. A break means that we take a break from each other. I don't think it's good for me to have you living under the same roof."

"I can sleep in the backyard then," I suggested. "Except for Mrs. Raymond's dog, who will sneak under the fence and lick my face all night. I don't know what flavor he thinks I am, but he sure likes to gnaw on my head bumps."

"I'm not asking you to sleep in the backyard, Buddy. What I'm saying is you need to go stay somewhere else. Having you here is a distraction from my work on the show.

An actor has to be calm and focused, and right now, having you here makes me uncalm and unfocused. Professionally speaking, of course."

"But where will I go?"

"You're so smart, Mr. Space Man. You figure it out."

The door slammed in my face and my heart sank. I had only had that feeling once before in my whole life, and that was when I had to say goodbye to Grandma Wrinkle when I left my home planet to come to Earth.

"Told you," Eloise's little voice said from down the darkened hallway. "She's tougher than math homework. You're toast, Buddy."

"Where am I supposed to go?" I asked her.

"How should I know. I'm only seven."

"Maybe your dad can take me to his place."

"Nope, he left a few minutes ago. Besides, tomorrow morning he's going on a business trip, whatever that is."

My head was reeling. Only a couple hours ago everything had been perfect. And now, everything was a total mess.

In my room, I flopped down on my bed and thought about my options. I could call Luis, but he was probably angry with me because I had abandoned him at the party too. I left him friendless and shrimpless. Obviously, I couldn't call Martha because I had ditched her along with Cassidy. I couldn't call Tyler because he hated me. That left Ulysses.

I picked up the new phone that Delores had bought for me with my first paycheck and called Ulysses.

"Hey, Buddy," he said. "How'd it go at the club? Was Cassidy great or what?"

"Bad topic, Ulysses," I said. "I didn't show and she's kicking me out of the house."

"Oh, that's bleak," he said.

"I wonder if there's any way I could come stay at your house temporarily until we can work this out."

"Mom!" Ulysses shouted. "Can Buddy come sleep over tonight?" He waited two seconds, then answered. "She said yes."

"I didn't hear her say anything."

"She always says yes. I can already hear her getting food out of the refrigerator to make us dinner. My mom's a one-woman feeding machine."

"Are you close enough for me to walk to your house?"

"No, but let me see if I can catch my dad. He's on his way home from our restaurant, and I bet he'll swing by to pick you up."

He put me on hold for a second, then came back on.

"Be waiting on the front porch. He'll be there in fifteen minutes. And when he says fifteen minutes, he doesn't mean sixteen. He's ridiculously punctual."

I sat there in the semidark room, in shock at what had just happened. Was I moving out for good? Was my friendship with Cassidy over? Should I take all the avocados out of the house or just the ripe ones? One thing was for sure, I had to start packing.

After I had put together all my things, I decided I should change back into my human form. I sat down on the bed and took hold of the amulet around my neck and started to chant.

"Be Zane. Be Zane Tracy now."

I didn't feel any of the electricity that comes when my body starts its biological alteration. It was so hard to concentrate because I was worried about being on time for Mr. Park. I had learned that lack of concentration really slows down biological alteration, but nevertheless, I couldn't get my brain to cooperate. When I saw Mr. Park's headlights coming up the driveway, I slung my duffel bag over my shoulder and crept silently down the hall to the front door. I paused at the door, and I looked back, hoping that Cassidy would come out of her room and tell me not to go.

She didn't, and I left.

11

The moment I stepped out of the car in front of Ulysses's house, a window from the second story flew open, and Ulysses stuck out his head. He was wearing a black cape and a Batman mask.

"It is I, the caped crusader," he shouted in a not-so-deep superhero voice. "Welcome to my bat cave."

Mr. Park shook his head and sighed as he helped me get my duffel bag out of the back seat.

"That kid," he said, "is going to have us evicted from the neighborhood. Last week, he tied a pillow onto our Great Dane and rode him down the street shouting, "Ride 'em, cowboy."

"Oh, I've seen a lot of old cowboy movies in black and white," I said. "My favorite one was when the bandits robbed the Pony Express."

"Why is a kid like you watching old movies?" Mr. Park asked.

"I used to watch all kinds of TV and old movies with my grandma on my planet . . ."

"On your planet?"

"I mean, on my couch. We like to call our couch the planet."

"It sounds like you and your grandma have a great relationship," Mr. Park said. "Family is at the center of everything. Come inside and take that costume off. Make yourself at home."

Mrs. Park greeted me at the door and opened the hallway closet. Taking out a hanger, she said, "You can hang your costume up here, Buddy."

"Oh, that's okay, Mrs. Park. The studio won't let me take it off unless there's a guard around. You know, the technology of my sensory enhancer is top secret."

"It's okay, Buddy, my good man," Ulysses said in an English accent, as he bounded down the stairs. "James Bond is here to protect your secrets. Just call me Bond, James Bond."

"I've seen those movies too," I said. "Secret agent, double O seven. He is so cool."

"Actually, I'm even cooler," Ulysses replied. "I'm Double O seven and a half."

Mrs. Park laughed and shook her head. "Ulysses has a big imagination. And a big appetite. Come into the kitchen, boys."

"Yeah, I'm starving," Ulysses said. "We usually eat earlier, and my stomach is growling like an angry tiger."

"Buddy, do you like Korean food?" Mrs. Park asked. "We're having barbeque beef and kimchi, specialties of the house."

I had never heard of kimchi, so I passed the word through my Earth language dictionary, which told me that kimchi is spicy fermented cabbage and radishes used as a side dish or main dish in Korean meals. That sounded interesting.

We sat down around their kitchen table and everyone took a bowl of beef and rice.

"What brings you to our house?" Mrs. Park asked, using chopsticks to put a heaping portion of kimchi into my bowl.

"I've been staying with Cassidy while my parents are . . . you might say . . . out of town. She and I had a little misunderstanding."

"Yeah, Cassidy misunderstood and thought you were a loyal friend," Ulysses said.

That stung, but deep inside, I knew it was true. An incredible wave of sadness swept over me. Mrs. Park reached out and touched my shoulder. Her hand was soft and kind, like Grandma Wrinkle's touch.

"Good friends have problems and then forgive each other," Mrs. Park said. "You two will work it out. Now, let's eat."

I picked up my chopsticks and holding them with all seven fingers, took a mouthful of kimchi from my bowl. It turned out those extra two fingers came in very handy, because everyone seemed surprised that I handled the chopsticks with no problem. It was only when the kimchi landed in my mouth that a problem developed. The dictionary had mentioned that it was spicy, but it didn't say exactly how spicy. It didn't say, "Buddy, when this stuff hits your taste buds it will set off an explosion in your body."

I was totally unprepared for what happened next. My two tongues felt like they were on fire and started slapping each other around in my mouth, trying to cool off. It sounded like a school of fish was blowing bubbles in there.

"Oh, we forgot to tell you," Ulysses said, laughing. "Kimchi has some kick to it."

When the kimchi passed through my throat and hit my stomach, my sensory enhancer objected and started to squirm. I pushed hard against the back of the chair to lock it in place, but it kept pushing me forward, and it looked like I was rocking in my chair.

"What's up with the rocking?" Ulysses asked. "Do you have to pee or something?"

"Yes, I do," I said, "so if you'll excuse me, I'll be back in a jiffy. Oh, and Mrs. Park," I gasped, not wanting to hurt her feelings. "You really make a delicious kimchi. Nice and spicy."

As I hurried off to the bathroom, I heard Mr. Park ask Ulysses about my sensory enhancer.

"How does he make that thing move?" he asked.

"Batteries, Dad. Six triple As."

The first thing I did in the bathroom was put my mouth directly under the sink faucet and gulp down as much water as I could in the hope that my tongues would calm down. My nose was running like a waterfall, and my sensory enhancer was jumping around frantically.

"That's it for you, pal," I said to it. "You've lost your kimchi privileges. I'm covering you up with human skin."

I sat down on the edge of the bathtub and took the amulet in my hand. I concentrated hard as I closed my eyes and chanted.

"*Be Zane,*" I whispered with intensity. "*Be Zane now.*"

I could feel my biological alteration going into action, and I started to relax. The eyes on the right side of my head shrunk down to one eyeball and my hair turned soft and human to cover my bumpy scalp. The long, spiny fingers on my right hand became Zane's graceful human fingers, and my suction cups retracted into five stubby toes. But then I became aware that my transformation to human was only one-sided. My right side was Zane, but my left side remained alien.

I tried to concentrate even harder to get my other half to cooperate.

"*Be Zane,*" I whispered. "*Be totally Zane.*"

The only thing I felt was the heat from the kimchi in my stomach rising up into a burning burp. I felt like I was breathing fire.

"Come on," I said to the amulet. "Do not leave me like this."

In desperation, I chanted as fast as I could, my voice rising to almost a shout.

"*Be totally Zane,*" I chanted. "*Both sides. Right and left. Be totally Zane.*"

My chanting was interrupted by a knock on the bathroom door.

"You okay in there, Buddy?" Ulysses said.

"Uh, I'm just having a little kimchi reaction," I said. "It helps to shout it out."

"Yeah, that happens to everybody the first time. I'll go get some ice cubes for you to suck on and bring them in."

"No!" I yelled. "Don't do that."

I couldn't let Ulysses see me in my half-alien, half-Buddy state. It would freak him out. In fact, it was freaking me out too. I looked down and touched my chest, at the spot where my human self joined my alien self. It hurt like crazy, as if my two skins were tearing apart from each other. I was a mess. My biological alternation seemed to be frozen, my stomach was on fire, my arms and legs were twitching in a blazing-hot kimchi dance, and my skin was about to split open. What was I going to do?

"I'll be fine," I shouted to Ulysses. "You go back to the table. I'm going to call Cassidy and apologize one more time."

"Good luck, dude," he said. "Girls can be stubborn. Not that I've ever talked to one. Except Martha. And she's stubborn."

When I heard Ulysses's footsteps fade down the hallway, I got out my phone and called Cassidy. She didn't pick up, so I called again. And again. And again. I must have called her twenty-five times. I was being ridiculously persistent, but I had no choice. I was in a panic. I was sick, hot, scared, and half-crazy. It felt like my alien side was at war with my earthling side. I needed a friend who understood my predicament, and let's face it, Cassidy was that person. I couldn't believe I had sacrificed our friendship for a dinner meeting.

On my twenty-sixth try, she picked up.

"What, Buddy?"

"Don't hang up. I really need you."

"I needed you but, oh right, you weren't there."

"I'm sick, Cass. Really sick."

"It sounds like your nose is running. My advice is to blow it. Good vnight, Buddy."

"No, wait! Don't go," I yelled into the phone.

I heard Ulysses's voice calling me from the kitchen.

"You okay in there, Buddy dude? Everything coming out okay?"

"I'm good. I'm fine," I yelled back. "I just dropped the soap dispenser on my toe. I'm going to soak it in the sink for a minute."

"Buddy, you're acting wacko," Cassidy said.

"Here's the thing, Cass. I'm in real trouble. My nose is running so much that it's actually made a puddle on the floor. But that's not even my worst problem."

"There aren't too many things worse than a puddle of snot."

"I'm frozen," I explained. "Half human, half alien. I think it was the kimchi that stopped my biological alteration."

"Kimchi? Are you at Ulysses's house? I've had his mom's kimchi. It's delicious but it packs a wallop. My lips were chapped for a week."

"I'm locked in the bathroom, Cass, and I need your help."

"What am I supposed to do? I'm not an alien doctor."

"You have to help me get to my spaceship. There's something there that I hope can save me."

"What could be there? We already opened all the compartments."

"Something in the toolbox. It's a long shot, but it might work."

"The toolbox? What are you going to do? Use a crescent wrench to tighten up your knees?"

"This isn't a joke. My body feels like I'm being torn in two, and it looks that way too. Please help me."

"I can't believe you're asking me for help after you hurt me so deeply."

"I'm sorry for what I did," I said. "You're my true friend, Cassidy. I know that now. And I'm not just saying that because I need your help."

There was a momentary silence on the phone, and I could almost hear Cassidy thinking. Suddenly, I felt a searing pain shoot down the front of my body.

"Ow!" I yelled, unable to help myself.

"What is it, Buddy?"

I looked down and saw purple blood start to seep from my chest where the alien me joined the human me. My body was literally splitting in two.

"I'm bleeding," I said. "And there's a lot of blood. Cassidy . . . Cassidy . . ."

I looked down at my phone. The screen had gone black. It was dead.

Was I going to be next?

12

I *didn't know what to do. I couldn't tell if Cassidy* had heard me. All I knew was that she was my only hope to help me stop the bleeding. My blood was flowing now, creating a purple splotch on my human and alien skin.

I tried my phone again, but it was dead. I couldn't go into the kitchen to use the Parks' phone on the wall. If they saw me in my half-alien, half-human state, they would call the FBI or the CIA or some other bunch of initials who would come and take me away.

My best plan was to sneak upstairs and see if Ulysses's phone was in his bedroom. I took one of the guest towels and held it tightly to my chest so I wouldn't leave a trail of purple blood on the floor. Quietly, I opened the bathroom door and crept over to the stairway. One of my suction cups made a popping nose as it hit the floorboards.

"Buddy, is that you?" Ulysses called out. "That's one epic bathroom visit you're having."

I stood perfectly still and didn't answer, until I heard Mr. Park say, "Ulysses, it's not polite to comment on people's bathroom habits. Buddy will return when he's finished."

"I'm just going to take my duffel bag upstairs and change into something more comfortable," I shouted into the kitchen.

Climbing the stairs was really difficult because of all the blood I was losing. I felt like I was climbing Vesta Mound, the tallest mountain on my planet, which is four times higher than your Mount Everest, which is 5.4990 miles high. For you nonmath types, that makes Vesta Mound 21.996 miles high. That's a lot of uphill miles when your legs feel like concrete.

Ulysses's bedroom was a show business fan's paradise. The walls were plastered with posters of all his favorite superheroes and movie stars. There were costumes and masks and hats hanging on hooks all over. Even the lamp on his desk was a glowing blue 3-D Iron Man face mask. I looked around for his phone, and I saw it lying on his desk, charging. Staggering over to it, I called Cassidy. It rang and rang, and finally she picked up.

"You have to get here now," I said.

"I am here. Almost, anyway."

"You are?"

"Yeah, I called Luis and he picked me up."

I went to the window and looked out to see Luis's car turning the corner.

"I'll be right down," I said. "Keep the motor running."

I opened the window and started to climb out. In my woozy state, I had momentarily forgotten that I was on the second floor and it was a long way down. I was going to have to take the stairs and somehow get out of the house without the Parks seeing me. I looked around the room for an idea.

The costumes! Thank you, Ulysses, for having the movie wardrobe of the century.

I took the Batman cape off one of the hooks and draped it over my body. It covered some of me, but not all of me. I turned it around so the cape would flow down my front and cover the bloody splotch. There was a pair of red Superman boots sitting in the closet, so I grabbed them and tried to stuff in my suction cups. That hurt so much, it gave me a lot more respect for Superman than I'd had before. It must be tough to fly when your feet are all bent out of shape.

I still had my head to deal with, which was half-human and half-alien. If the Parks saw that, they would freak out for sure. I tried Ulysses's Batman mask, but it only covered the top half of my face, so that wasn't going to work. Hanging on a hook next to it was a big, round astronaut's helmet with a blue visor. It even had a microphone attached. I slipped it over my head, pulled the visor down, and tried out the mic.

"Testing, one, two, three," I said.

The amplifier inside the helmet made it sound like there

was another person in the room. I wasn't prepared for the loudness of my voice.

If walking up the stairs was hard, going down was even harder in my too-small superman boots. My suction cups were practically screaming, "Let me out of here." I clutched the towel tightly to my chest, holding the cape over it so no one could see my purple blood. At the bottom of the stairs, I called out into the kitchen.

"I'll be going now," I said and edged toward the front door, hoping I could just sneak out. Mr. and Mrs. Park weren't about to let that happen. They got to me faster than a marathon runner crosses the finish line.

"Where are you going?" Mrs. Park asked.

"And why are you dressed like that?" Ulysses added.

"Cassidy called and said there is a special scene we have to rehearse tonight."

"That's weird," Ulysses said. "I never heard about a new scene."

"It's our musical number for the show, and she's come up with a new twist to surprise Duane. She wants me to sing backup."

"And you're doing it my superman boots?"

"Yeah, they're so tight that they help me hit the high notes."

Fortunately, there was a knock on the front door. Mr. Park opened it, and Cassidy was there, smiling her most charming television-star smile.

"Hi, Mr. Park," she said. "We're here to pick up Buddy. Luis and I have a craving for cheeseburgers, and Buddy said he wants to come along. You know, he didn't get the name Buddy Cheese Burger for nothing."

"But I thought you guys were going to rehearse your musical number," Ulysses said.

I tried to give Cassidy a knowing look, but she couldn't see my eyes through the blue visor. She's so smart that she picked up on the story anyway.

"Right!" she said. "We're going to rehearse at Rocket Burger. It's the best cheeseburger stand in all of Hollywood. There is something about their chocolate milkshakes that really loosens up your vocal cords."

"That's very odd," Mr. Park said. "Bordering on incomprehensible."

"They are traveling into another dimension," Ulysses said in a fake, eerie voice. "Into the mysterious territory between light and dark, known only as Milkshake Zone."

"Ulysses, can you be serious for a minute?" Mr. Park seemed annoyed. "Your mother and I need to know that Buddy is safe."

"I assure you we're safe," Cassidy said. "Luis is very responsible."

"Are you coming back to sleep here tonight?" Mrs. Park asked.

"No, I'm not."

"Yes, you are," Cassidy said.

"But I assumed I was going back home," I said, giving her a quizzical look.

Cassidy took a deep breath. "Buddy, I came here because that's the right thing to do, but I haven't forgiven you."

Wow, that hurt. Right then and there, I promised myself that I would try to make it right with Cassidy, if I survived the night, that is.

I said goodbye to the Parks, thanked them for everything, and told them I'd see them later. Luis was waiting on the porch to help Cassidy get me down the driveway to his car.

"Do you want to ride shotgun?" he asked. "Muriel has some good beats coming out of her speakers."

"I have to lie down in the back seat," I said. "And the only beat I want to hear is my heart."

"Whoa, this sounds serious," Luis said. "Where are we headed?"

"To my spaceship," I moaned. "And fast."

13

To be honest, I barely remember the ride to the back lot. I took off the cape and tied it tightly around my chest to try to stop the bleeding. Cassidy had to help me remove the astronaut helmet, because my arms were too weak to even lift the visor. The only thing I specifically remember was relief when Luis pulled off the red Superman boots. My suction cups practically cheered with joy to be once again free.

When we drove up to the front gate, Cassidy stuck her head out the window and smiled at the guard.

"Hey Gil," she said. "We just need to pick up some geography homework that we left behind. Our set teacher is going to give us an F if we don't finish."

"Geography is tough," Gil said. "If you need help, I can name all five of the Great Lakes. Let's see . . . there's Huron and Ontario . . ."

"That's okay, Gil. We're in kind of a hurry."

"I'll tell you the other three on the way out," he said. "And don't dawdle, because I'm kind of bending the rules to let you kids on the lot."

I must have let out a moan from the back seat, because Gil put his face up to the window and asked, "Do you have a puppy back there?"

"That's just our pal Buddy," Luis said. "He had too much kimchi for dinner."

"Kimchi's delicious. Your pal Buddy needs to get a stronger stomach. Now off you go."

He raised the parking gate for us, and we sped off, passing the commissary and soundstages and prop warehouses until we reached the back lot tour area. Luis knew all the nooks and crannies of the lot and parked his car in a special space that was used for recharging the staff golf carts. I could see my spaceship parked next to the hamburger stand where I'd landed only six weeks before. I hoped there was something waiting for me inside it that would put a stop to the bleeding and return my powers of biological alteration.

Cassidy held me under one arm and Luis under the other and practically dragged me to the spaceship. It had become a fixture on the back lot, with tourists just assuming it was part of a film set. We were the only three people in the world who knew that it had made the journey to Earth all the way from a distant red dwarf planet.

"Open the hatch, Cass," I said, my voice wavering.

Cassidy climbed up the ladder and pulled on the handle. "It doesn't open, Buddy."

"Oh, I forgot. You have to enter my password on the keypad next to the hatch. It's S-K-Y-W-A-L-K-E-R."

"I never knew you were a *Star Wars* fan too," Luis said. "Give me a high five, bro." I held up my hand to Luis and he grinned. "I guess I should have said give me a high seven."

My Skywalker password worked like a charm and the hatch clicked open. Cassidy climbed into the small cabin. I draped myself across Luis's back, and he carried me up like a firefighter rescuing a person from a burning building. When the three of us jammed inside, there was no room for us to move at all.

"Now what?" Cassidy asked.

"Look under the pilot's seat," I instructed her. "There should be a silver toolbox there."

Cassidy wiggled around so she could lift the cushion, and sure enough, there was Grandma Wrinkle's toolbox. Cassidy lifted it out and handed it to me. I took a deep breath before I unlatched it, hoping that it would contain the special tape we use on my planet to repair everything from metallic liquid hydrogen tanks to cuts in our outer layers of skin. We call it Kapton tape.

A wave of disappointment swept over me when I saw there was no tape in the toolbox. There was an industrial-strength nail clipper, which we have to use twice a day to keep our nails from curling around our elbows. It was just like Grandma Wrinkle to put an extra one in because I was always losing mine. There was a crowbar for prying open spaceship doors and a titanium hammer for breaking up meteorites. There were drills and clamps and voltage meters, but no Kapton tape.

My heart sank.

"It's not in here," I whispered.

"What are you looking for?" Luis asked.

"The Temperature Stability Kapton tape."

"Oh, is that the outer-space version of the double-sided scotch tape we use to wrap Christmas presents?" Luis asked.

"It can seal anything," I said. "I was going to use it to close the wound before my alien and human selves split in two."

"Like a gigantic, super-powered Band-Aid," Cassidy said. "That's a great idea."

"It would have been a great idea if it were in here, but

it's not." My head was spinning and my hands were shaking. The tape had been my last hope of survival.

"Okay, let's all calm down and take one more look," Luis said. "My grandma always says seek and ye shall find. I'm going seeking."

With that, he wiggled the entire cushion of the pilot seat free and stuck his hands deep into the hole below it.

"What do you feel?" Cassidy asked.

"Well, my right hand is feeling my left hand. Oh, wait a minute. Way down here in the corner is something round and sticky."

"That's it," I said. "Get it up here right away."

"I can't reach it, dude. I can only touch it with the tips of my fingers. Cassidy, hold my ankles. I'm going in."

With Cassidy holding his ankles tightly, Luis lowered the upper half of his body into the dark space under the seat.

"Got it!" he exclaimed.

He emerged with a big smile and a full roll of Kapton tape. I was so happy to see it that I even managed a weak cheer. Even my sensory enhancer, which had wilted like a flower in a cosmic heat wave, gave a little yip.

"Okay, guys, I'm going to need your help," I said. "Pull

off a long strip of tape and cover the wound from top to bottom."

"There's a lot of blood there, dude," Luis said. "I get nauseous at the sight of blood, especially purple blood. I hope I don't barf on you."

"Luis, this is life and death," Cassidy said. "No barfing allowed. Here, give me the tape."

She pulled off a strip of tape about six inches long and struggled to tear it from the roll.

"I can't rip it," she said.

"There are nail clippers in the toolbox," I said. "Find them fast. Please hurry."

Luis rummaged around and came up with the extra pair of industrial-strength nail clippers Grandma Wrinkle had sent.

"Cut here," Cassidy said, holding out the strip of tape.

Luis made the cut successfully, but then the tape stuck to the nail clippers. When he tried to pull it off, it stuck to his fingers.

"Luis, stop fooling around," I said.

"You try this," he said. "This stuff is stickier than peanut butter on the roof of your mouth."

Cassidy reached out and peeled the tape from his fingers, and then she placed it gently on my chest wound. Almost immediately, I heard a crackling sound up and down the cut. That could mean one of two things. Either I was healing completely or completely coming apart. The three of us stared at my body, waiting to see what would happen next.

I'm glad to report, friends, that Kapton tape lives up to its reputation. If you ever find yourself in a situation where your human self is separating from your alien self, run (don't walk) to get yourself a roll of Kapton tape.

The tape was strong enough to hold the two sides of the cut tightly together, and within a minute, healing started to take place. The layers of my skin closed around the wound and the bleeding stopped. Then an even more miraculous thing happened. Right in front of our eyes, the tape dissolved as if it had never been there. My wound was gone. I felt my strength returning. Even my sensory enhancer perked up and started to sniff Luis.

"Hey, keep your snout off the merchandise," Luis said. "Go sniff somewhere else."

My sensory enhancer let out a little snort that was not altogether friendly. But even so, I was glad to see it coming back to life.

"Wow," Cassidy said, still staring at the spot where my wound had magically healed. "That was amazing."

"I've got to find out what's in that tape," Luis said. "We

could make a fortune right here on Earth selling it on TV. I can just see the infomercial now—I'll do the pitch, and Cassidy, you can be my assistant."

"Uh, Luis. Let me just point out for a minute who has her own television show and who doesn't. I'll do the pitch and you'll be *my* assistant."

"But I had the master plan."

"Guys," I said. "While you discuss your future fortunes, I have some more immediate business to take care of. This half-and-half thing isn't working for me, so if you'll excuse me, I'm going to try to become whole. You might want to look away."

I took hold of my amulet, closed my eyes, and felt my newfound strength course through my body.

"*Be Buddy*," I chanted. "*Be the* whole *Buddy. Be Buddy now.*"

The healing Kapton tape had allowed my powers of biological alteration to take full effect, and I was relieved to feel my human half transforming into Buddy. Three eyes became six, the hair on the left side of my head receded and was replaced by my bald bumps. The stubby toes on my left foot returned to their original suction cup selves. My sensory enhancer felt alive again. I was becoming one hundred percent my alien self.

When I was fully restored, I opened all my eyes and rotated them in a complete circle to make sure they were in working order. They landed on Cassidy and Luis, who were staring at me with their mouths agape. Until that moment, I hadn't realized they had never actually witnessed my complete biological alteration in progress.

"Dude," Luis said. "That was incredible, and I mean in a really disgusting way."

"I think what Luis is trying to say," Cassidy added, "is that watching you transform was like watching that scary scene in *The Swamp Creature*—the one where a thousand eyes pop out all over his body . . . but times a million billion trillion."

"I'm not sure if that's a compliment or an insult," I said, "but I'm going to go ahead and just say thank you."

We opened the hatch and, one by one, climbed down the ladder. This time I didn't need any help. The three of us headed across the food court area for the secret space where Luis had parked his car, not too far from Strawberry Supreme, the ice-cream stand that sells what they call the strawberry-est ice cream west of the Mississippi. The stand itself is even shaped like a large strawberry ice-cream cone. As we passed by, I stopped dead in my tracks. I was not prepared for what I saw.

Parked next to Strawberry Supreme was a spaceship very similar to mine. I hadn't seen it there before. Had I just missed it? Unlikely. Surely I would have noticed.

"Have you ever seen this spaceship before?" I asked Luis.

"No, it must be new. I'll bet they had the props department build one to look just like yours."

"Probably," Cassidy agreed, "because your ship has become so popular. Everyone lines up to see it."

Of course, I thought, *that must be what it is*. Everyone wants to see a faster-than-light vehicle. And the props department did a very good job of making this one so realistic.

We walked over to the spaceship, and I reached out to touch the shiny silver exterior. It was warm, and I could see pale smoke coming from its engine. A glowing yellow light flickered from the porthole window. Wait, were those footsteps I heard coming from inside the cabin?

No, it couldn't be.

But then the hatch opened, and I saw a woman's silhouette looming in the doorway. My sensory enhancer reached out toward the woman. It sniffed the air, then let out a low growl.

"Hello, Citizen Short Nose," the woman said, flashing me her crooked smile.

"How do you know my name?"

"Oh, I know many things about you," she said. "You've certainly been a pain to track down, but there you are and here I am. And this time, there's no one to protect you."

She laughed, and I cringed as the night filled with the awful sound of someone choking on a chicken bone.

14

Luis and Cassidy stared up at the figure in the doorway of the spaceship.

"Wait a minute," Cassidy said to her. "I know you. You're that photographer who burst onto our stage and hid in the tree."

I looked closely and realized that Cassidy was right. The woman at the spaceship door had a blond ponytail with a black ribbon and those same glowing cat eyes.

"You're only half right, my little television princess," the photographer said. "I am that photographer, but I can also be anyone else I want to be."

As the woman descended the ladder of the spaceship, my sensory enhancer crept up around my neck to get a closer whiff of her. The photographer glanced at it and didn't seem in the least bit alarmed. In fact, she went right up to it and poked it with her finger.

"Don't you act up," she snarled, her words shooting into the snout of my enhancer. "I can finish you off whenever I want. And you know I will."

Upon hearing her words, my sensory enhancer slithered down my back in retreat.

"Anyone interested in seeing my new necklace?" the photographer asked. "Cassidy, I'm sure you like jewelry."

"Uh, yeah, I do," Cassidy said, "but this seems like a weird time for a fashion show."

"Actually, it's the perfect time."

The photographer pulled a necklace from under her shirt and flashed it in front of us. It looked a lot like my amulet. In fact, it was almost identical.

"Hey, where'd you get that amulet?" I asked.

"Oh, it was designed by a certain old woman I know," she said. "You might know her too. Watch what it can do."

She clutched the amulet tightly and right before my six eyes, her face and body melted away, and she transformed into the guy in the club with the spiky hair and olive-green mesh tee shirt—the one with the mean eyes.

Luis and Cassidy stared, their jaws dropping almost to the ground.

"Did you see what I saw?" Luis said. "That woman became a dude."

"It's the guy from the Nike party," Cassidy whispered. "Isn't it, Buddy?"

"Yes and no," I answered.

I was starting to understand what was going on, and the thought filled me with terror. This strange person, whoever she was, had somehow gotten access to Grandma Wrinkle's secrets. The amulet, the biological alteration, the transformation into many human shapes—these were all Grandma Wrinkle's inventions.

When my sensory enhancer saw the guy in the tee shirt, it shot out from my back and started to swipe at him. The guy reached out and punched my sensory enhancer right in the snout, and I felt the pain run all the way down my spine. With a yelp, my sensory enhancer slumped over, unconscious, and hung lifelessly off my back.

"You're a real bully, dude," Luis snapped, shaking his head in disgust. "You should pick on things your own size."

"It was warned," the guy said, then reached for his amulet again.

"Let me see that," I said, trying to grab the amulet from around his neck. He pushed me away, and he wrapped his hands around the amulet. I could hear him chanting under his breath, and within seconds, his spiky hair faded away and turned into a baseball cap. The rest of his body followed, transforming into the uniformed gas man who had mysteriously showed up at Cassidy's house.

"Does this ring any bells?" the man said with a sneer, his eyes glowing in the darkness.

"Buddy, what is going on?" Cassidy said. "This is too weird for me."

"Biological alteration," I whispered.

My blood ran cold as I realized what I was observing. This was not a human. This was a body-snatching alien sent to Earth to find me.

"Are you from my planet?" I asked.

"Yes, I am," came the answer. "Before I left, we took a very lovely tour of your Grandmother's subterranean cave and found lots of interesting things. Illegal things, like movies and television and art and music."

"Oh, so you know how great those things are," I said, hoping for the best. "And now you've come to help me?"

The man in the uniform threw down his clipboard and laughed out loud, that choking sound again, as he took another step toward us.

"Let me introduce myself," he said, clutching the amulet. "My real self."

As he clutched the amulet, his human face and uniformed body melted away, leaving a steamy cloud of yellow mist, from which emerged a large, muscular woman with six eyes, a bald bumpy head, and suction cups for feet.

"Buddy, this is so freaky," Cassidy said. "It's another you."

"Only a girl you," Luis added.

"I'm no girl, you ignorant human," the alien said. "I am a commander in the elite Body Snatching Corps of the Squadron. My name is Citizen Cruel. I think that says it all."

"Can I just say that right now, my mind is blown in so many pieces, I'm never going to be able to put it back together again," Luis said.

My mind was racing. My first thought was that if this woman had been in Grandma Wrinkle's house, she would have information about her.

"Have you seen my grandmother?" I asked. "Is she okay?"

"She's alive, if that's what you mean. Last time I saw her, she was in a glass cage, nice and cozy. Or as cozy as you can be when you can't stand up."

She let out that laugh again, raspy and mean.

"Citizen Short Nose, your grandmother is one of us now. She has given us lots of useful information. Like the formula for this amulet. And the plans for building a space-ship. And of course, the coordinates for how to get to this particular spot on Earth."

"I know Grandma Wrinkle, and she wouldn't give

you that," I said. "She would never cooperate with the Squadron."

"Oh, you're so right, Citizen Short Nose. But after we injected her with a brain relaxer, she suddenly became very talkative."

Citizen Cruel took a step toward me, her yellow eyes glowing with a cold fire.

"It's time for you to come home, Citizen Short Nose." Her voice was steely and heartless. "The Supreme Commander wants to have a word with you."

I certainly did not want to have a word with him. And deep down, I didn't believe anything this puppet of the Squadron was telling me about my grandmother.

"Can you give the Supreme Commander a message for me?" I said. My voice was quivering even though I was trying to act brave. "Tell him I'm doing really well and I'm on a TV show and if he'd like to come and see it, I can get him free VIP tickets."

"Hey!" Luis whistled. "I didn't know you could get VIP seats. You never got those for me."

"Guys," Cassidy whispered. "Not now. In case you haven't noticed, the alien lady isn't amused."

I got deadly serious.

"Although I appreciate you going so far out of your way

to come here and escort me home," I said to Citizen Cruel, "I don't want to return to our planet. Life is good for me here."

"Citizen Short Nose, you are as stupid as the back end of a dung beetle," she snarled. "I am not *inviting* you to return. I am *telling* you that if you want to see your grandmother alive again, you will come with me now. Have I made myself clear?"

"Not entirely," I said. "I'm hoping that there is room for negotiation. I learned how to do that in Hollywood. Like when I first got my own dressing room, I asked for three kinds of ice cream in the freezer. The studio was only willing to give me one, so I said okay, but it had to be butter brickle."

"What kind of drivel are you spouting?" Citizen Cruel hissed. "This is not about ice cream, whatever that is. This is about an illegal intergalactic escape."

"You might think my escape was illegal, but Grandma Wrinkle and I felt it was a matter of my survival."

"Oh, and would you like to see what your Grandma Wrinkle thinks now? She is sorry she ever encouraged you to leave."

Citizen Cruel shoved her arm in front of my face and pulled up her sleeve, revealing a watchlike device on her wrist. Its screen glowed bright yellow.

"Whoa, nice watch," Luis said. "Can you get texts on that?"

"You and your paltry human technology," Citizen Cruel scoffed. "Can you get holograms on yours?"

She pushed a button on the device. Suddenly the screen on her wrist filled with Grandma Wrinkle's face, which rose out of the screen into an actual 3-D image floating in the air before our eyes.

"Is that your grandma?" Cassidy asked. "Wow, she has more wrinkles that an elephant's ankles. She should moisturize."

"Let's see how great you look when you're 987 years old," I said.

I would defend my grandmother against anyone. Her face may be wrinkled, but it was beautiful to me. I was so glad to see her that I reached out and tried to touch her— but my hand went right through the hologram.

"We can't actually touch, my beloved grandson," the hologram said, "but you can see and hear me. Listen carefully to what I have to say. It is time you return home to our wonderful planet with its kind rulers who care about your well-being."

This was not sounding at all like something Grandma Wrinkle would ever say.

"But, Buddy, I thought you escaped from your planet because the leaders were so awful and repressive," Cassidy said.

"Silence your pathetic single tongue," Citizen Cruel

snapped at Cassidy. "You are being disrespectful to one of our wise elders."

"Grandma Wrinkle," I said to the hologram. "Tell me. What do you want me to do?"

"Give up your ideas about freedom," the hologram responded. "Come back and set an example by supporting our government. Our home planet cannot tolerate those who follow their senses, who listen to their imaginations. From now on, you must always do as you're told. Just like Luke Skywalker did."

The second I heard those words, a flash of recognition shot

through me, like an alarm going off in my head. To Grandma Wrinkle and me, Luke Skywalker was a hero. We always talked about how he never went to the dark side, how he fought evil no matter what. He would never have given in to a repressive and cruel government. This was not my Grandma Wrinkle speaking.

"Okay, Grandma Wrinkle," I lied. "I will come home."

Citizen Cruel nodded in approval. "I knew the old bat would talk sense into you. You will come with me now."

"I just need to get into the compartment in my spaceship where I keep my spare amulet," I said, thinking fast. "I don't want to leave it behind for an earthling to get their hands on. But so much has happened on Earth that I've forgotten the compartment password Grandma made for me. Can I ask her for it?"

"You may," Citizen Cruel said. "But say nothing more."

"Grandma Wrinkle," I said. "Can you tell me what our special password is?"

"Of course, grandson," the hologram said. "Our password is K-L-I-N-G-O-N."

My password with Grandma Wrinkle was S-K-Y-W-A-L-K-E-R. We used it for everything because it stood for all that was good in the universe. K-L-I-N-G-O-N would never have been our password, and when I heard Grandma Wrinkle say that, I knew for sure she was sending me a message to make it look like she was cooperating. On one of our favorite Earth television shows called *Star Trek*, the Klingons were evil and ruthless, qualities that Grandma Wrinkle fought against her whole life. And here she was, secretly letting me know she was still fighting.

It all became clear. The Squadron had stolen Grandma Wrinkle's formula for the amulet and the scientific plans for the faster-than-light vehicle. They had forced her to make the hologram trying to convince me to come home, but she had outsmarted them. Now Citizen Cruel had been sent to kidnap me, to rip me away from my new life and take me back to my planet, where I would be imprisoned or who knows . . . even worse.

I knew I had to get away. But how?

I had my brain run a search of the preprogrammed ideas for a quick escape that I had seen in all the movies I'd watched. Run for the door. Take a hostage. Fake being sick. Put up a distraction. That was it—a distraction!

I pointed to the hamburger stand behind Citizen Cruel and used all my new acting skills to shout, "Uh-oh, there are two guards coming toward us and they look fierce!"

Citizen Cruel whipped her head around to look in the direction I was pointing.

"Run!" I hollered to Cassidy and Luis. "Run like the wind."

I took off across the food court, remembering to run on my tiptoes so my suction cups wouldn't slow me down. Cassidy and Luis followed, and we zigged and zagged around the churro stand, past the taco truck toward Strawberry Supreme. Citizen Cruel followed us in hot pursuit, her large feet so powerful that her suction cups pulled up chunks of pavement as she ran.

"You can't outrun me, you earthling insects," she yelled.

Her voice sounded mechanical and magnified, piercing the night air and reverberating in my ears. I knew she was using the voice amplifier that all members of the Squadron had implanted in their throats. I had heard that awful voice before, when I was trying to outrun the Squadron while escaping from my home planet.

I had thought our knowledge of the ins and outs of the back lot would give us a tremendous advantage, but Citizen Cruel's physical powers were too much for us. As we approached Strawberry Supreme, she caught up to us and reaching out, grabbed Cassidy around the waist.

"I've got you, you slow little snail," she croaked, wrapping her long, spiny fingers around Cassidy in a crushing grip.

"Buddy! Luis! Help!" Cassidy screamed.

We turned and saw Cassidy battling Citizen Cruel, struggling to get free.

"Your puny little punches merely tickle me." Citizen Cruel laughed. "Is that all you've got, earthling?"

Luis and I ran to Cassidy's rescue, each of us grabbing one of Citizen Cruel's legs and tugging to try to knock her off her feet. But her suction cups were so powerful that they held her

legs like steel rods cemented into the ground. Even though we yanked on her legs with all our strength, she remained upright. We slugged her in the calves, bit her in the knees, thumped her in the thighs, but nothing we did had any effect.

Holding Cassidy in one hand, Citizen Cruel grabbed Luis by the hair and tried to lift him off the ground, but he had so much gooey product in his hair, he slid right out of

her grip and landed on the pavement. She reached down and wrapped her seven fingers around the back of his neck, then lifted him into the air like a toy.

"You two human pests are annoying me," she cackled. "It's time to get rid of you!"

"No, I don't want to die," Luis said.

"Me either!" Cassidy cried. "I'm singing for the first time in this week's show."

"You earthlings are so unimaginative," Citizen Cruel snorted. "There are many things worse than death. But for now, I just need you out of my way."

Shaking me off her leg like a dog shakes off fleas, she took a few giant steps to the Strawberry Supreme ice-cream stand. She yanked open the door at the bottom of the cone and shoved Cassidy and Luis inside. Just opening the door for a split second filled the air with the scent of strawberries—there must have been hundreds of crates of them stored inside for making fresh ice cream. Citizen Cruel slammed the door shut with her foot, and then she did something I had never seen before, even on my planet. Without flinching, she snapped off one of her long fingernails, which had grown to at least eight inches in length, and used it as a bolt to lock the door.

"That will never hold," I said to her, trying to pull the latch open.

"You know better than that, Citizen Short Nose," she said. "Our fingernails are stronger than titanium."

She was right. Our fingernails are almost indestructible, which is why we have to use our industrial-strength nail clippers several times a day to keep them in check. Otherwise, they become dangerous even to ourselves.

From inside the ice-cream cone, Luis and Cassidy pounded on the walls, shouting in panic. I could hear all those crates of strawberries toppling off the shelves. Even over the clatter, I could still hear their voices.

"Buddy! Save yourself! Get away from her!" Cassidy shouted.

"Dude, we'll be okay," Luis yelled. "There's enough strawberries in here to survive for a month. Now beat it!"

Citizen Cruel reached out to grab me. I knew I couldn't overpower her, but neither could I let myself be captured. I wouldn't return home. I couldn't. Never.

I had to resort to the most basic escape plan ever invented. Running.

I tucked my head down, filled my three lungs with air, and ran for my life.

15

I **took off across the back lot, heading for the area**
where they shoot all the exterior scenes in movies. At
Universal, there are entire city blocks that range from typ-
ical suburban streets to villages in Mexico to the old-time
streets of New York. I figured that the New York street
would give me the most places to hide, because it was full
of apartment buildings and fire escapes and movie theaters
and diners and shops of all kinds.

I ran so fast that for the first time in my life, my three
lungs were not enough. Even with my third lung pumping
as much air into my body as it possibly could, Citizen Cruel
overtook me with ease. She must have had enormous lung
power because when she caught up with me in front of the
Lyric Movie Theatre, I was gasping for breath and she was
barely panting.

"Your attempt to escape is laughable, Citizen Short

Nose," she said, grabbing me by the neck and pinning me against the brick wall. "There is nowhere for you to go."

Glancing around, I saw that I was leaning against the movie theater entrance, and I realized that if I could just escape her grip and get inside, there would be many places to hide—under the seats, in the manager's office, behind the popcorn counter. Citizen Cruel was nose to nose with me, and I could detect the musty scent of our planet's nutritional wafers on her breath. My sensory enhancer certainly detected it too, because suddenly I felt it coming back to life. It took one sniff of her and snorted wildly.

"Oh, it's you again, is it?" Citizen Cruel said. "I thought I had made it clear that you are to keep still."

She curled one hand into a fist, or as close to a fist as her long fingernails would allow her to make, and she threw another punch directly at my sensory enhancer. It squealed and passed out again. The pain from the punch shot through my entire body, and I opened my mouth and let out a loud wail. The kimchi must have still been rolling around in my digestive tract, because when the breath came out of my mouth, it was like a dragon breathing fire. My spicy kimchi breath blasted directly into Citizen Cruel's face, and I saw her six eyes nearly bulge out of her head. Her red lips curled back, and she broke out into a coughing fit. While she was doubled up, I backed into the entrance of the theater and slammed the door shut.

I turned around to look for a place to hide. The first thing I noticed was that I was not inside at all. When I looked up, I saw the Hollywood hills and blue sky above me. Of course, I should have realized that the movie theater was fake. In fact, all of the New York street was fake. There were only fronts of buildings, supported by wooden beams in back. Like everything else on the back lot, this was Hollywood movie magic, but this time, the magic wasn't working for me. I had no popcorn counter, no manager's office, no place to hide.

I went back to good old reliable Plan A, which was to keep running.

I didn't intend to run back to the food court, but I was so panicked that I didn't look where I was going and found myself heading in the direction of the Strawberry Supreme stand again.

"You're running in circles," Citizen Cruel shouted as she pursued me. "Just like one of those fluorescent bearded rats from Planet Zeno. You can't escape me, you little rodent."

I could hear Luis and Cassidy in the ice-cream cone stand, pounding on the walls. They were pounding so hard that the entire cone was wobbling from side to side. If only I

could make it there, perhaps I could help tip it over and free them. The three of us together had a chance of overtaking Citizen Cruel.

But Citizen Cruel was too fast for me, and before I could reach the ice-cream cone, she tripped me and pinned me to the ground with her suction cup feet. I found myself compressed like a pancake against the concrete.

"I have a suggestion," she said, pushing her foot hard against my chest. "Why don't you be a good little citizen, quit all this running-around nonsense, and just get your pitiful broken body into my spaceship. This cat-and-mouse game is starting to bore me."

I tried to wriggle free, but I couldn't move. Her gigantic suction cups were smothering me. I glanced down to check if the Kapton tape was still holding me together. The last thing I wanted was to start spurting blood.

I had my brain search for more escape options, but this time, it didn't produce anything useful, only images of escapes from sunken pirate ships or zombie attacks or evil giant insect infestations. I was out of moves.

16

"Let's get this show on the road, shall we?" Citizen Cruel said, curling back her red lips to show me her crooked, gummy smile. "I've had enough of this ridiculous planet Earth and its shallow inhabitants."

"If you stayed here a while, you'd see that the people are really warm and helpful," I said. "Not cruel and heartless like the Squadron."

"Well, my little rat, you'll have plenty of time to reflect on your warm memories when you're locked forever in your prison pod. That is, if the Supreme Commander lets you live."

Citizen Cruel grabbed both of my legs and started to drag me over to her spaceship. My sensory enhancer was just conscious enough to feel the pain and moaned with each step.

"Your poor little enhancer," Citizen Cruel said. "Look

how it's suffering, and it's all your fault. You should have deactivated it on your thirteenth birthday like every other citizen and put it out of its misery."

"Then I would be an unfeeling robot with no spark in my life, just like you," I managed to spit out. If I was going down, at least I was going to go down standing up for what I believed.

"Talk all you want, Citizen Short Nose, because as soon as we get back to our planet, your sensory enhancer will be deactivated and of no use to you ever again."

As she dragged me along the pavement to her space-ship, I suddenly heard a thunderous crash like the sound of a small building collapsing, which is exactly what it was. Luis and Cassidy had managed to tip over the Strawberry Supreme stand. The round, pink strawberry scoop that had been the roof of the stand had tumbled off and was rolling across the food court, crashing into Luigi's Pizza. From the corner of my eye, I saw Luis and Cassidy, splattered with red strawberry juice, scrambling to crawl out of the cone.

"Over here!" I yelled.

They looked all around to see where my voice was coming from, and when they spotted me, Cassidy got to her feet and held out her hand to help Luis.

"I twisted my ankle," I heard him say.

"You've got to tough it out," she said to him. "Buddy's life is on the line."

Citizen Cruel yanked me even harder toward the spaceship.

"Hurry!" I called to them. "She's kidnapping me and taking me back to my planet."

"We got you," Luis yelled.

He bent down and picked up two metal ice-cream scoopers that had scattered on the ground when Strawberry Supreme fell over, and he tossed one to Cassidy.

"What am I supposed to do with this?"

"Be creative," he said. "It's the only weapon we've got. You use that one, and I'll take the double scooper."

Luis hobbled over to the path and got down on his knees next to the shrubs.

"Watch out," he hollered at Citizen Cruel. "We're coming after you."

When Citizen Cruel saw Luis digging in the dirt next to the shrubs, she let loose one of her chicken-bone laughs.

"What do you children plan to do with those deadly ice-cream scoopers?" She sneered. "Oh, I'm so afraid."

Actually, she had a good point. In the history of weapons, ice-cream scoopers are very low on the list. As a matter of fact, I'm pretty sure they're at the bottom.

"You're laughing now, but watch this," Luis shouted at Citizen Cruel.

He stood up and pointed his ice-cream scooper at her. It was loaded with the pebbles that surrounded the shrubs. Aiming directly at Citizen Cruel, he catapulted the pebbles at her, and they shot through the air like missiles. He had a good aim, and several hit her body.

"Oh, now we're throwing baby rocks," she said. "I'm trembling."

"Wait until you see what I have," Cassidy yelled.

She grabbed one of the tubs from the toppled-over ice-cream stand and filled her scooper. As she tossed the ice cream with all her might at Citizen Cruel, we could see chunks of strawberries flying through the air. The scoop landed with a *thunk* smack in the middle of Citizen Cruel's face. Some even dribbled into her mouth.

"Nice toss," Luis yelled to Cassidy. "Right in the strike zone."

"What is this junk?" Citizen Cruel yelled, spitting out the ice cream. But before she could finish the sentence, her mouth started to twitch violently. Then her body shook as if she had been hit by a bolt of lightning.

"Forget the pebbles, let's load up on the ice cream," Cassidy said, observing Citizen Cruel's reaction.

She and Luis filled their scoops with more ice cream and flung it directly at Citizen Cruel. One scoop, two scoops, followed by a triple scoop, until her face was covered with strawberry ice cream. You could see the chunks of strawberry sliding from her eyes to her chin.

I felt Citizen Cruel's grip on me start to weaken, and as I looked up into her face, I saw that her eyeballs were turning bright red. At first it was just eyeball numbers three and four, but within seconds, all six of them were a flaming scarlet red.

I recognized what was happening. She was having the same allergic reaction to strawberries that I had. It must be some imperfection in our DNA. Her tongues flapped around in her mouth, desperately try-ing to stop the unstoppable itch that I knew was overtaking her. And then it happened.

"I can't see," she shouted.

Cassidy answered by tossing another scoop directly in her eyes.

Citizen Cruel batted blindly in the air with one hand, and I took the opportunity to break free from her grip and sprint over to my friends.

"Buddy, look!" Cassidy said. "She's got the same allergy you do."

"Now's our chance," Luis said. "I'm going in."

In a move that would make any professional basketball player jealous, he hurled himself through the air, reaching out for Citizen Cruel and grabbing her around the knees. That brought her to the ground. Then Cassidy and I jumped on top of her and held her down. She was still moaning and swinging her arms blindly in the air.

"Take my sweatshirt," Cassidy said, untying it from around her waist and handing it to me.

"Thank you, but I'm not cold," I said.

"No, use it to tie up her legs. She can't walk if her ankles are tied together."

As I wrapped the sweatshirt around her ankles, I held my breath so my allergy to the strawberries wouldn't flare up. Cassidy rubbed her hands all over Citizen Cruel's face.

"What are you doing?" I asked.

"My hands are covered with strawberry juice. I'm just giving her an extra dose."

Luis took off his belt and handed it to me.

"Wrap this around her wrists," he said. "If my pants start to sag, don't look."

Luis joined Cassidy in holding Citizen Cruel down. She couldn't fight them off, because she couldn't see where they were. I took the belt and tried to grab her wrists, but in her wild flailing, she accidentally punched me in the nose. Her punch packed a wallop, and when I reached up, I felt some purple blood trickle from my nostrils.

"I'll thow you," she tried to say. "You can't out-thmart the thquadron."

Her tongues were so swollen, they barely fit in her mouth, but I understood what she was saying. Her words only made me more determined to show her that she and her evil Squadron would never control me. But she was strong, and Luis saw that I needed help.

"I'm going to give her a mega-shot of strawberry," he said.

He took his tee shirt, which was covered with smashed strawberries, and put it over Citizen Cruel's nose so she had no choice but to breathe in all the strawberry fumes. She groaned, and as she took several deep breaths, I could feel her body weaken. I wondered if she might die because I could see her life force starting to dwindle.

As I finished tying up her wrists with Luis's belt, she looked up at me with her bright-red eyes and muttered something that sounded like "squishy fish eyes." Then she seemed to pass out.

"I can't understand her," Cassidy said. "It's like when you got so weak and kept saying those weird things."

"Yeah, about reindeer poop pellets," Luis said. "You didn't make any sense."

"I actually did make sense," I protested. "Reindeer really do poop pellets, as do rabbits and squirrels."

"Buddy, do we really need to hear your random collection of facts right now?" Cassidy said. "We have to get this alien out of here before she comes back to herself."

"Let's get back into her spaceship and blast her off to where she came from," I said. "Everyone agreed?"

"Does that plan sound good to you, missy?" Luis asked Citizen Cruel playfully.

"Yes, my commander," she muttered. "I will do whatever you ask."

"Cool," Luis said, his eyes suddenly full of fun. "Can you cluck like a chicken?"

With all her remaining strength, the once-powerful Citizen Cruel burst out into a raucous chicken imitation, clucking her confused brains out.

"Bwak . . . bwak . . . bwak . . . BWAAACK! BWAAAAACK!"

Luis and I couldn't stop laughing, but Cassidy was annoyed.

"I can't believe you guys." She shook her head. "One minute you're in mortal danger, and the next minute, you're laughing like a couple of two-year-olds."

"You're right," I said. "Luis, you grab her arms, I'll take her legs, and Cassidy, you support her middle. Let's get her to the spaceship."

With Citizen Cruel continuing to cluck like she was laying an egg, we dragged her the rest of the way across the food court and over to her spaceship. By the time we pulled her up the ladder and shoved her into the cabin, she was limp as a wet noodle. Luis and Cassidy strapped her into the passenger seat, and I directed my attention to the controls on the dashboard.

"We're in luck," I said, looking at the digital display that lit up when I touched the screen. "The coordinates to my home planet are already programmed in."

"So all we have to do is fire this baby up, and she'll take

off across the galaxy for home?" Luis said. "What genius thought that up?"

"My grandmother. She was the master mechanic of our starfleet and truly is a genius."

"Okay," Cassidy said. "She's strapped in and ready for takeoff. You all set, Buddy?"

Luis and Cassidy climbed out of the cabin and descended the ladder.

"I'm sending you back," I said to Citizen Cruel. "And don't ever return." And then, just in case she could hear me, I added, "And you better be nice to my grandmother. She's a powerful person and deserves respect."

I leaned forward and pushed the ignition button with my long fingernail.

"Have a nice trip," I said, stepping out of the cabin and slamming the door shut. As I jumped to the ground to join Luis and Cassidy, I was grateful for my suction cups that gave me a soft landing on the pavement.

We heard the spaceship engine rumble and watched as smoke billowed out of the engines. But before I could have the pleasure of watching Citizen Cruel blast off into outer space forever, I heard the blare of sirens coming our way.

"Oh no!" Cassidy said. "The police. That's not good."

"But we haven't done anything wrong," I said.

Luis shook his head. "How about trespassing? Breaking and entering? Being on the premises after hours? Destroying a giant strawberry ice-cream cone?"

"I see your point. Therefore, I vote once again for running."

"It's unanimous," Cassidy said.

The three of us took off and headed for Luis's car. We ran in the opposite direction of the sirens, and never so much as turned around to look back. When we reached the secret parking space, we piled into the car and pulled out so fast the tires squealed like we were on a motor speedway.

"I don't hear the sirens anymore," Cassidy said as we sped across the lot to the exit.

"I hope that means that she had already taken off and they didn't find her," I said. "I want her gone forever."

I looked up to see if I could spot Citizen Cruel's vehicle shooting across the sky. I thought I saw a flickering light moving in the direction of Mars, but it was so far away, it could have been a shooting star.

As our car reached the gate, we slowed down and waved to Gil, who was still on duty.

"Look normal, everyone," Luis said. "Except for you, Buddy. You just look like your usual weird self."

Luis pulled to a stop in front of the guard shack and greeted Gil.

"You guys okay?" Gil asked. "There's some kind of commotion going up at the food court. I hear the wind may have tipped over the Strawberry Supreme ice-cream stand."

"We didn't hear anything," Luis said. "Stage 42 isn't anywhere near there. And anyway, we wouldn't have heard anything because the soundstages are soundproof."

"Good point," Gil said. "I hope you found your

homework. Oh, and by the way, I remembered the other Great Lakes. There's Superior, of course, and then there's . . . wait a minute . . . I just had it on the tip of my tongue."

He paused and rubbed his chin. Meanwhile, all my eyeballs were rotating 360 degrees around my head to make sure no police cars were following us.

"Give me a minute, kids," Gil said, reaching into his pocket. "I'll look it up on my phone."

We had no time for this, so I ran Great Lakes through my brain processor. I had the answer nanoseconds later.

"There are five Great Lakes," I blurted out from the back seat. "Huron, Ontario, Michigan, Erie, and Superior."

"There you go," Gil said. "You got a lot of info in that kid brain of yours."

Yes, I thought, *if he only knew how much was packed in there.*

"Thanks for all your help, Gil," Luis said. "I have to get these kids home."

With a friendly wave, Gil raised the gate and we took off into the night.

As we drove off the lot, we were all silent, still stunned from our close encounter with Citizen Cruel. Even Luis, who is usually calm and cool, was visibly shaken. When he turned the corner onto Ventura Boulevard, he cut the turn too close and bumped into a streetlamp.

"Oh no," Luis said, pulling over to the curb. "I hope Muriel is okay. I keep her in perfect condition."

Cassidy unhooked her seat belt and jumped out of the car to inspect the damage.

"Sorry to say, Luis, but Muriel has a nice little dent in her fender," she reported.

"Oh man," Luis groaned as he joined Cassidy on the sidewalk. "What am I going to do? I can't afford another expense, but I can't let Muriel drive around wounded."

"I think I can help." I climbed out of the back seat, stepped onto the curb, and saw that the dent was about the size of a watermelon.

"I want each of you to hold me tight around the waist." I instructed Luis and Cassidy. "I'm going to need both my feet for this."

While they held me, I lifted up both legs and positioned my suction cups over the dent on the fender.

"All right, pull me back as hard as you can," I said.

They did and we all heard a pop as the suction from my feet pulled the fender back to normal.

"Whoa," Luis said. "That was unbelievable. I can't thank

you enough, Buddy. And if Muriel could talk, she'd say the same thing."

We got back in the car, and a huge wave of exhaustion swept over me.

"I'm ready to go home," I said.

"Correction," Cassidy said. "You're ready to go to Ulysses's house."

In the excitement of the evening, I had forgotten that I was still banned from Cassidy's house. You would think that all the danger and threat would have softened Cassidy, but apparently that was not the case. As we drove back to Ulysses's house, none of us said a word. We were all lost in our own thoughts.

But no matter what each of us was thinking, there was one thing we all shared and that was the memory of fighting off Citizen Cruel together and sending her back home.

We had come face to face with a monster, and we had won.

17

I *spent the night in the top bunk of Ulysses's bunk bed.*
I had the hardest time sleeping I've ever had in my life.
You're probably thinking that was because I was haunted by
nightmares about Citizen Cruel, but in fact, what kept me
up all night was Ulysses. He does voice impressions in his
sleep. Every few minutes he was somebody else. He went
from imitating Donald Duck to Adam Sandler to Abraham
Lincoln. He even did most of Martin Luther King Jr.'s "I
Have a Dream" speech. Even though it kept me from sleeping, I found it very inspiring.

The next morning, Mr. Park left early for work and
dropped me off at Cassidy's house so I could get a change
of clothes. Delores was sitting on the porch having her
morning coffee while Cassidy and Eloise were getting ready
inside. Delores was wrapped in a blanket, although I don't
know why she needed it, because she was so red-hot angry, I

thought I saw steam coming from her ears. The minute I got out of the car, she jumped out of the chair and said, "Come inside, mister. I need to have a word with you and Cassidy."

She got Cassidy from her room and sat us both down at the kitchen table. Then the interrogation began. Cassidy just sat there with her head in her hands, staring at me angrily. It didn't seem to matter that we had shared a terrifying night together—she was still plenty mad. Delores's questions came fast and furious.

"Where were you last night?" she ranted, pacing back and forth.

"I slept at the Parks' house."

"Without letting me know where you were going?"

"You might say it was a spur-of-the-moment decision. Cassidy knew where I was."

That was the wrong thing to say, because Delores immediately turned to Cassidy and fired a barrage of questions at her.

"So now I know where he was, but I still have no idea where you were. Tell me, missy, where were you and why were you out so late? And why didn't you call? How could you do this to me? Didn't you know I'd be worried sick? What kind of child puts her poor mother through this? What did I do wrong? How did I raise such an irresponsible ingrate?"

I had never heard the word *ingrate*, so I ran it through my Earth dictionary and found that it meant "an ungrateful person."

"Oh, let me correct you, Delores," I said. "Cassidy might be irresponsible, but she is not an ungrateful person. She says thank you to everyone and appreciates all that they do for her. I've noticed that on the set."

Now Delores was glaring at me.

"Here's a show business tip for you," she said. "Don't ad-lib when I'm talking. Just imagine the camera's on me now."

"But there is no camera here, Delores. Oh wait, is it hidden in the cabinets?"

"Buddy," Cassidy said, "what my mom is saying is that you're not helping the situation and you're definitely not helping me."

"Cass, you know I want to help you in every way I can. I'm always here for you."

"Yeah, like last night. It was great to see you in the audience at the club. Oh wait, you're the best friend who wasn't there. Thanks so much for showing up."

"See what I mean, Delores?" I said. "Listen to how Cassidy said thank you to me. She is such a grateful being on this planet."

"Buddy, I was being sarcastic," Cassidy said. "Apparently you missed it."

She went to the refrigerator and poured herself a glass of orange juice. I got the water pitcher from the top shelf, filled it to the brim, and chugged down every last drop. It had been an exhausting night, and I needed all the hydration I could get.

"Buddy," Delores said. "How many times have I told you not to drink out of the pitcher?"

"I would have to say eighteen," I answered. "Unless you count the time you told me not to drink from the faucet. That would make it nineteen."

"I give up," Delores said. Then turning to Cassidy, she resumed her attack. "You still haven't answered my question, Miss Cassidy Louise Cambridge. I need an explanation of where you were last night."

"Well," Cassidy said, taking a long sip of juice very slowly so she could think of an answer. "After the club performance, Luis dropped Martha off at home and we drove to Ulysses's house to pick up Buddy. Then we went to the studio to get our geography homework, which we had left behind. I knew you would approve of that, Mom."

"Why? Since when have I been a fan of geography?"

"But you always tell me I have to get good grades to stay on the show," Cassidy answered. "Those are your exact words. And taking those words very seriously, we went to Luis's grandmother's restaurant to study. I knew you would approve of that too."

"Why would you go to a Mexican restaurant to study when you have a perfectly good desk in your own room? You're not making sense, Cassidy."

Oh boy, I thought. Cassidy was painting herself into a corner of lies. But she rose to the occasion.

"Actually, Mom, our geography quiz is on Latin American countries. And as it turns out, Luis's grandmother knows a whole lot about the geography of Mexico. She was very instructive."

The look on Delores's face was somewhere between suspicious and confused. I decided to step in and help.

"For instance, Delores," I chimed in, "did you know that

Guadalajara, Mexico, is the tenth-largest Latin American city in population. We learned that last night."

"You know who's not interested?" Delores said, waving her red fingernails in my direction. "Me. Population of one."

"Mom, can we finish this some other time?" Cassidy said. "Today is camera day. Martha and I are doing our song for the crew so they can work out all the camera angles, and I need to get ready."

It was brilliant of Cassidy to bring up our long work day. That's the one thing that would get Delores off our backs. She was all work and no play.

"Well," she said, "you will have close-ups, and I certainly don't want to be responsible for you having rushed through your makeup regime. We'll postpone this conversation until later when I have decided what consequences I intend to dish out. And trust me, there will be consequences."

"Delores, how about if you eliminate the consequences this time?" I suggested in my friendliest tone of voice. "Cassidy was very stressed last night."

"Really?" she said. "Memorizing a few facts while munching on chips and salsa? You call that stressful?"

"I sure do," came a little voice from down the hall. It was Eloise, in her unicorn pajamas, who had wandered out from her bedroom. "Salsa can be really spicy and stress out your tongue. That happened to me once. I had to suck on an ice cube and then I got a brain freeze."

"Now look what you've done," Delores sighed. "She's going to be talking about her tongue injury all day. Eloise, you need to get dressed right now. You've got until the count of three to go pick out your school clothes."

"I can count to three in Spanish," Eloise said. "*Uno, dos, tres . . .*"

"That's great," I said. "I can count to three in almost every language except Hungarian, which is really hard for me."

"Cool," Eloise said. "Let's do it now. I have lots of time."

"No one here has any time," Delores said. "Not for Spanish, not for French, and definitely not for Hungarian. It's time to get dressed. Eloise, come with me."

She took Eloise by the hand and led her down the hall to her room. The door slammed behind them, and I could hear them arguing about whether Eloise was going to wear her hair in one braid or two.

"I don't have time for this," I heard Delores say. "Just wear a hat."

Cassidy stood up to go to her room. She seemed to have nothing to say to me, but I knew we needed to talk.

"Are you okay?" I asked her. "You saw some pretty scary things last night."

"I certainly have a lot to process," she answered. "That always seems to happen when I'm with you, but last night was epic. That alien woman was right out of a horror movie. Only for real."

"She's gone," I said, "and we're safe. But now you understand how awful the Squadron is and why Grandma Wrinkle made sure I escaped."

"She must be such a brave woman to resist them," Cassidy said. "I really hope she's all right."

"So do I. And by the way, you were really brave last night too, Cass. Without you by my side, I would be on a spaceship to prison right now."

"I'm glad you're not."

"Does that mean you forgive me for not being at your performance?"

"You really did hurt my feelings. I thought I could count on you."

"You can from now on."

"You'll have to prove that, Buddy. Right now, it's just words. Words are easy. Actions are hard."

"You'll see, Cass. I'll be the best alien friend any human could ever dream of. I'm so grateful that you decided to show up to rescue me. You were a true friend. And I hope you'll let me come home."

She stood there for a long minute, thinking. My heart was pounding. I wanted her so badly to say yes.

"Rebuilding trust takes a while," she said finally.

"Is that a yes or a no?"

"It's a yes but not a total yes."

"Does that make it a maybe."

"No, Buddy. Maybe is maybe."

"Okay, I'm not following," I said.

"You can come back and live here, and I'll try to forgive you, but you have to show me that you can be a better friend."

"I will. Just watch me."

As we stood there in the kitchen, I looked out the window at the rooftops of the houses in the valley below us. In the distance, I could see Universal Studios up on the hill. I remembered how, on my home planet, that place had always seemed like a distant dream to me, and now, it was my home away from home. And this house, with my friend Cassidy, was my safe haven on Earth.

At least, that's what I thought.

18

After I had a quick soak in the tub and got dressed, I made myself a robust breakfast of thirty-eight avocados, packing in all the nutrients I'd need for the day. Cassidy made herself two Pop-Tarts, but when Delores saw that, she intercepted them and put them in her purse.

"Have an orange instead," she said to Cassidy. "It's only ninety calories. Pop-Tarts are no good for you."

"If they're so bad, how come you're putting them in your purse for you to eat later?"

"Am I the one on camera?" Delores said. "No. I'm only eating them to save you. See how I'm always looking out for you?"

After breakfast, I noticed a pain in the center of my chest. At first, I thought it was indigestion from the last eight avocados. (Here's a tip for you: If you're having avocados for breakfast, stop at thirty. Those last eight will throw your digestive system into a tizzy.) Then I started to worry that the Kapton tape we had applied the night before had not held and the wound in my chest was pulling apart again.

Cassidy grabbed her backpack and headed for the car. Delores was already in the driveway, arguing with Eloise about why she had to sit in her booster seat.

"Buddy, hurry up," Delores called. "If you're late, it's a bad reflection on me as your manager."

"I'll be out in a minute," I hollered. "I have to do one quick thing."

I raced down the hall into my room, slammed the door, and opened my spacesuit to inspect my chest. I could see the remains of the glue where the Kapton tape had been. Although the wound was still closed, the skin around it was a darker blue than the rest of me and surrounded by dried patches of purple blood. I didn't want to take a chance that the wound would rip open again, so I decided to transform into Zane. My human skin would act as a body bandage and hold my two sides solidly together until I was completely healed.

I sat down on my bed, took hold of my amulet, closed my eyes, and started to chant.

"Be Zane. Be Zane now."

A horn honked impatiently from the driveway.

"Buddy," I heard Delores yell. "Get the lead out of your suction cups. We don't have all day."

I had to block all distractions—her voice, the sound of the engine, the repeated car honks—but I was able to do that and my biological alteration went off without a hitch. Within seconds, I was Zane Tracy, teen idol with slicked-back wavy hair, two eyes, and a set of human feet.

"I see you took your costume off," Delores said as I slid into the back seat. "You should give it to the wardrobe department to send to the dry cleaner. It's getting a little fragrant, if you get my drift."

"I did a lot of stress sweating last night," I said. "I was really scared."

"Scared about what? A little geography quiz?"

Cassidy put her fingers to her lips, letting me know that she would handle the conversation.

"What Buddy means, Mom, is that geography is scary. Think about it. There are 195 countries in the world, and we're supposed to remember the capital of every one of them. Talk about scary."

"I know what you mean," Eloise agreed. "I'm scared about my spelling test today. I have to know how to spell tongue. It's got lots of silent letters. If you ask me, it's too long."

"So is your own tongue," Cassidy said.

"Yeah, but I can touch the tip of my nose with it," Eloise answered. "I bet you can't do that."

"I bet I can."

They spent the rest of the ride to Eloise's school trying to see whose tongue could stretch the farthest. I wished I could tell them about my two tongues and the amazing things I can do with them. I can touch my eyebrow with the upper one while touching my chin with the lower one. But I was stuck in my Zane body, and my human tongue can't do anything but hang out in my mouth.

After we dropped Eloise off at school, we drove to the studio where Delores let us out at the door to Stage 42. It was going to be a long day. On Thursdays, we act out all the scenes in front of the crew. Duane decides where the four cameras are placed, and the camera operators mark their position with different-color tape on the stage floor. On our set, Jose on Camera One uses red tape. Beth on Camera Two uses yellow tape, while Jamal on Camera Three likes green. Freddy on Camera Four uses blue tape because he says it matches his eyes.

Cassidy and I took our cast chairs in front of the cafeteria set. It still thrilled me every time I got to sit in that blue canvas chair with Buddy Burger written on the back in big white letters. Martha joined us, sliding into her chair next to Cassidy.

"Are you ready for our big song?" Cassidy whispered to her.

"Yes, we're ready," Martha answered.

"We? Who's we?"

"I meant to say me," Martha said.

"Of course you did. I get it. You're nervous. Me too."

Cassidy threw her arm around Martha and gave her shoulder a reassuring squeeze, but then pulled her hand away quickly.

"Ow," she said. "Martha, you gave me a shock."

"Martha, have you been dragging your feet on a carpet?" I asked. "That friction will cause the buildup of an electrical charge on the surface of an object, a phenomenon known as static electricity."

"You don't always have to show off, Buddy," Martha said, with a sour expression. "Everyone knows that. It's second-grade science."

It wasn't like Martha to say something so grumpy, but I just chalked it up to her nervousness.

"Okay, kids, let's get started," Duane said. "I want to begin by blocking the big talent show scene. Where's Ulysses?"

"I'm here, boss," Ulysses said, running onto the set, carrying a Tupperware container. "Sorry I'm late, but my dad left early so my mom had to drive me, and she insisted on sending kimchi for everyone to share at lunch."

Still holding the kimchi container, he flopped into his chair. Despite the lid on the Tupperware tub, the odor of kimchi wafted up and curled under my nose. That stuff was so spicy its aroma could penetrate lead. Even though it was tucked tightly under my human skin, my sensory enhancer started to wiggle. Suddenly it let out a shriek that sounded like my back was screaming. Everyone turned to stare at me, so I immediately opened my mouth and let out another shriek to cover the sound.

"Dude, what's wrong?" Ulysses asked.

"Oh, I'm warming up my vocal cords," I answered, trying to sound casual. "You know, just like Martha does all the time. Show them how you do it, Marth."

Martha opened her mouth and let out a shrill squeak that sounded liked "Eek . . . eek . . . eek." It made the hair on my human head stand on end.

"Wow, that's not like any warm-up I've ever heard you do before," I said. "What happened to do-re-me-fa-sol-la-ti-do?"

"I'll warm up my chords the way I want to," Martha snapped, "and I'll thank you to butt out."

"What's with her?" I whispered to Cassidy.

"She's just nervous about our number," Cassidy whispered back. "Give her a break."

Duane handed the new script pages to each of us. They

were printed on goldenrod paper, which told us that they
were the final changes.

"You'll notice that the writers worked all night to incor-
porate yesterday's changes," Duane said. "As you recall, Tyler
was upset with all the . . . shall we say . . . physical comedy
that was in the script, so we took that down a notch, and we
gave him a more mature, very important part. By the way,
where is Tyler?"

"We just got a call that he's arriving on set now," Jules,

the assistant director, said. "He had another event this morning."

"He knows I don't tolerate tardiness," Duane said. "What kind of event would be more important than rehearsing a hit show that tapes in front of a live audience tomorrow?"

He had a real edge in his voice.

"I say fire his pretty-boy face," Martha snapped.

"Whoa, Martha," Ulysses said. "You sure woke up on the wrong side of bed this morning. Lighten up. Tyler may be a pain in the neck, but he's one of us."

We heard a flurry of activity outside the door of the soundstage, and then it opened and a shaft of light shot in.

"Don't worry, everyone. I have arrived," said the shadowy figure at the door.

Of course it was Tyler, making his usual star entrance.

He sauntered up and took a seat in his blue canvas chair.

"You can start now," he said to Duane as he took the goldenrod pages from Jules.

"Why, thank you," Duane said. "And would it be too much if I asked where you've been that made you late for rehearsal?"

"While you little worker bees were poring over your little lines, I was at the opening of a mini-mall in Tarzana, where my many fans were gathered."

"Twelve does not constitute many," Duane said, unimpressed.

"There were more than twelve."

"I'm not interested," Duane snapped.

"Perhaps this will interest you, then," Tyler said. "I cut the ribbon for the opening of Big Mike's Pizza Parlor. I don't want to brag, but we had heavy press coverage."

Ulysses burst out laughing and held up an imaginary microphone in front of Tyler's face.

"Tell me, Mr. Stone," he said, using the voice of a TV anchorman. "Our sources have learned that you prefer a thick crust to a thin crust. Can you confirm or deny these rumors?"

Cassidy and I cracked up. Martha just sighed with annoyance, but Tyler turned red in the face.

"Okay, you laugh," he said. "But I don't see that any of you has a Big Mike's pizza named after you. That's right . . . the pizza with pineapple and red pepper at Big Mike's Tarzana branch is now called The Tyler Stone Special. Eat your heart out, kids."

"Sounds like the pizza will take care of that," I said. "I have heartburn just from the thought of pineapple and red pepper."

Ulysses, Cassidy, and I were having a great time poking each other in the ribs and laughing, but Duane was not amused.

"Might I remind everyone that we have a lot of work to get done today," he said. "Tyler, if you look over your pages, you'll see that we've made a lot of adjustments to your part, in light of your complaints from yesterday."

"I'm assuming that you've returned me to the leading role as host of the talent show, and I applaud your choice. It's a role that's going to let me shine."

"Well, that's not exactly what we did," Duane said. "Why don't you look over the revised pages while we put the show on its feet for the cameras."

"Why would you put a show on its feet?" Martha said. "It doesn't have any feet."

That made me think of weeks before, when I first arrived on Earth and heard that expression. I asked the same thing, but it was strange that Martha was asking it now. She had already been on the show for a year, and in show business since she was a little singing toddler doing diaper commercials.

"What's up with you? Are you having a memory lapse?" I whispered to her.

"How about if you mind your own business," she said, scowling at me so hard there were wrinkles all up and down her face.

I had heard of actors getting a bad case of nerves before

a performance, but Martha's anxiety seemed to have gotten the better of her. I decided to be a good friend and let her remark go.

"You're going to do fine," I said, giving her a reassuring pat on the arm. She must have still had some static electricity running around in her, because I got a shock too.

The shock was no big deal, but what was a big deal was Tyler's reaction to the new pages. He turned purple and blue and threw the script on the floor and, as usual, stood up and stomped off the set.

When you read the scene, I think you'll understand why. Here it is.

19

INT. CAFETERIA — DAY

The Oddball Academy students are in the midst of performing the talent show for parents' weekend.
PRODUCER'S NOTE: BUDDY THE ALIEN is still the host. TYLER sits in a director's chair over on the far-right corner, with his back to the audience.

                    TYLER

    Action!

                    BUDDY THE ALIEN

    Welcome to our talent show, where Oddball Academy students compete to show off their unique skills. The winner receives a luxurious trip to Uranus. The runner-up gets a

year's supply of toothpaste AND a
bright-yellow toothbrush in their
choice of soft, medium, or firm.
Don't lose it, you only get one.

Tyler turns to the audience and holds
up the toothbrush, flashing his bright
smile. A sound effect PINGS on his
bright, white front tooth.

BUDDY THE ALIEN

Our first act is a duet by our very
own Cassidy and Martha. Put your
hands together as the blended voices
of the Carrot Tops fill our cafeteria with music. Cassidy and Martha.

Cassidy and Martha come out dressed as
carrots. The greens look like they're
sprouting from their heads.

CASSIDY

Hello, ladies and gentlemen. We'd
like to sing our own composition, a
little ode to the food here at Oddball Academy cafeteria. We're calling it "Do Chickens Have Nuggets?"

Cassidy and Martha burst into their song.

CASSIDY AND MARTHA

Macaroni, crunchy fish sticks

*Chicken nuggets, cheese on
toothpicks*

*Puts us in a hungry mood
To close our mouths and chew our
food.*

CHORUS:
*Lunchtime, snack time
Dinner too
We gather here
To chat and chew.*

Buddy and Ulysses come to center stage
and take their places behind the singing
duo. They break into a rhythmic dance
step while snapping their fingers and
singing backup.

BUDDY TAND ULYSSES

Ooo . . . wah . . . ooo . . . wah
Chat and chew . . .
Ooo . . . wah . . . ooo . . . wah
Me and you.

Martha and Cassidy dance along with Buddy

and Ulysses for the big chorus line finish. The music swells, Buddy holds for
the applause, then takes the microphone.

BUDDY THE ALIEN

Thank you, Martha and Cassidy. You
are two of the most talented carrots I've ever heard. Not that I
spend a lot of time talking to
vegetables. And now, ladies and
gentlemen, we'll take a brief in-
termission to change the scenery
for our next act, Ulysses Park,
who will be doing his impression
of Joan of Arc's horse rolling in
the mud. And now, let's hear from
our director.

TYLER
(with his back still to the audience)

Cut!

GO TO BLACK

20

Duane was steaming mad that Tyler stomped off the set, and he sent Jules to fetch him from his dressing room. We heard Tyler return to Stage 42 before we even saw him.

"I reread the new scene, and it's worse than the original one," he bellowed as he crossed the stage. "First you have me swinging from a rope and getting slimed, and now you have me sitting with my back to the audience, saying nothing."

"That's not true," Duane said. "You have two important lines."

"Correction. I have two words," Tyler said. "*Action* and *cut*."

"And those are two very important words," Duane answered. "In fact, my job depends on them."

"This is not the character that I signed up for, Duane. And trust me, my fans will not stand for it. You will be hearing from them."

"You know what they say, Tyler," Ulysses said, trying to ease the tension. "There are no small parts, only small actors."

"Yeah, you would know, pip-squeak."

"Hey, hey, hey," Cassidy said. "You can't go calling Ulysses names. We're an ensemble. And if we don't have good chemistry together, the show doesn't work. The audience will feel that for sure."

"And why do you think we have an audience?" Tyler answered. "They're watching me, not you, and certainly not that alien creep standing there with his eyeballs twirling and his trunk snorting."

We stood there with our mouths hanging open, all of us but Martha, that is. She burst out laughing and said, "You have a point there, Tyler. Buddy and his bad Halloween costume are ruining the show."

"Martha!" Cassidy said. "What are you saying? You love Buddy. Just the other day you were telling me how funny he is and how much he adds to the show."

"Well, I've changed my mind." Her voice sounded cold and distant, not like the Martha we all knew.

"Listen, kids, I've seen this kind of conflict before," Duane said, "and it tears a cast apart. It's called professional jealousy. When one member of the cast takes off in popularity, it's good for the show, but at the same time, it's hard for the other actors not to feel jealous. I think that's what's going on. Is that what you're feeling, Martha?"

"My feelings are none of your business, Duane. Why don't we just move on? I'm going to memorize my lines so we can finish this up and get out of here."

Martha took the script and held it up to the side of her head, just like I do when I read.

"What are you doing?" I asked. "Are you making fun of me?"

Martha looked surprised and stammered for a minute before she answered.

"Yeah, I am making fun of you. It's so strange that you hold the script up to your head. Makes you look like a dork."

Duane rubbed his eyes and the back of his neck at the same time.

"We're not going to accomplish much in this kind of mood," he said. "Let's take a five-minute break so you guys can get your act together. Martha, go back to your dressing room and find a smile. And Tyler, you have to be a professional and do what the script requires. This is about what you can do for Oddball Academy, not what it can do for you."

"Okay, everyone," Jules called out. "Let's take a hard five."

I knew Martha and I had to talk this out. She had become a good friend, a person who was full of life and music and joy. Professional jealousy didn't seem natural to her.

"How about if we go to the craft service table and get something to drink," I suggested to her. "We need to talk."

"I don't know about the talking part, but I like the drinking part," she said. "I'm still so thirsty. Last night I must have consumed ten gallons of water."

"Why?"

She stammered a little before she answered, then said, "Oh, I must have had too many potato chips. Yes, it was definitely the potato chips."

When we got to the craft service table, Mary gave me my usual big welcome.

"Hey, Buddy, step right up. I just made some fresh guacamole for you. I know how you love your avocados."

"Avocados?" Martha asked. "Is that something you eat a lot of?"

"You know that, Marth," I said. "I love guacamole. It tastes great and gives me tons of energy. It's full of vitamin K."

"Right, I know you like guacamole. I just didn't know about the vitamin K. Mary, do you have enough for me too?"

"Well, that's a surprise," Mary said. "You've always told me you don't like anything green."

"People can change their minds."

"They sure can, honey," Mary answered. "I can't give you much, because I have to save it for my boy Buddy here, but I'll give you a small scoop and some chips. You're going to love it."

"I think I'm especially going to love the vitamin K."

Martha and I took our snack, and I suggested we sit down on a couple of folding chairs. I gobbled down my guacamole in three mouthfuls, and I watched as she tasted hers. She seemed to like the taste and licked her lips with pleasure. This is rude to say, because I know you shouldn't criticize a person's appearance, but I couldn't help noticing that her tongue looked really weird, like it took up a lot of her mouth.

"What are you staring at?" she snapped.

"See, that's what I want to talk to you about." I was glad to get the conversation going. "Everything you're saying today is kind of rude and, to be honest, mean. You're hurting everyone's feelings."

"Why should I care about anyone else's feelings? And as for you, stop wiggling your butt so much when you're dancing backup during my song. I see you trying to hog the spotlight."

"Martha, you're doing it again. I'm not sure what's gotten into you, but I know one thing. We're friends, and we have to be there for each other no matter what. I just learned that the hard way with Cassidy. You remember how I wasn't there for her at the club, or for you either for that matter."

"What club?"

"You know, the Silverlake Café. The other night?"

"Oh, right. Now I remember. Shame on you. That was terrible."

"I apologized to Cassidy, and now I'm apologizing to you. From now on, let's be friends and go back to work with a whole new attitude. And I promise I'll watch my wiggle."

I reached out to give her a hug, but she had already turned her back to me and was heading over to Mary for more guacamole.

"That stuff makes me feel great," I overheard her say to Mary. "From now on, I want as much as Buddy gets. And don't forget it."

"Well, listen to you, little Miss Diva," Mary said. "You know better than to talk like that. Especially to me, who makes sure there are always your favorite chocolate peppermint patties in the freezer."

Martha didn't answer, just headed back to the set. Mary shot me an annoyed glance, shrugged her shoulders, and said, "Looks like everyone's having a bad day."

We started rehearsal in the cafeteria set, holding our new

goldenrod script pages. It didn't go well. Tyler kept getting up from his director's chair to move the performers around as if he were really directing the scene. Every time Duane told him to sit back down, he said he was expressing what his character would really feel.

"Feel less, sit more," Duane said to him.

When it came time for Cassidy and Martha to do their song, the problems got even worse. Martha couldn't stay on tune, and her voice sounded screechy like a knife scraping across a plate. It was all I could do not to put my fingers in my ears.

Duane got so frustrated he was ready to pull the ponytail off his head.

"You know what, gang," he said, gathering us all together. "We're spinning our wheels here, and the show is getting worse rather than better. I'm going to make an executive decision to call off the rest of the rehearsal. Martha, you go home and rest your voice. Tyler, you go home and find the best performance you can do sitting down. Buddy, you have a lot of new lines to learn. I want you to be off-book tomorrow."

"What about me, boss?" Ulysses said. "What should I do?"

"You and Cassidy are perfect, and you get the rest of the day off."

"Cool," Cassidy said. "There's a *Star Wars* marathon on TV. I'll call my mom to come get us."

"Not so fast," Janice, our set teacher, said. "I graded your algebra test. You got ninety percent."

"That's good?" Cassidy asked hopefully.

"No, you got ninety percent wrong," Janet said. "If I were you, I'd skip the TV and go home and study."

"I can help you," I offered. "I'm good at algebra. I learned it in preschool."

"Yeah, with the other little nerds," Tyler said.

"Okay, enough with the name calling," Duane said. "Everyone go home and prepare for tomorrow's dress rehearsal and taping. I'll see you here at nine o'clock."

Delores came to pick us up and as we drove home, Cassidy suggested we stop for ice cream.

"The answer is no," Delores said. "Actually, twice no. No, because ice cream is not on your diet. And no, because you'll be busy cleaning out the garage."

"You're kidding, right? Mom, television stars don't do that."

"The ones who stayed out late without calling their mother do. I told you there would be consequences."

"Don't worry, Cass," I whispered to her. "I'll do your half of the work."

"Why would you do that?"

"I told you I was going to be the best alien friend a human being could ever have."

She smiled at me and that made my purple blood feel very warm.

As we pulled into the driveway, Cassidy's phone rang.

"Who is it?" I asked.

"I don't know," she answered. "There's no number on the screen. That's odd."

Cassidy started to answer the phone, but Delores held out her hand.

"You can give that to me, young lady," she said. "No phone privileges until the garage is done."

Delores took the phone and held it to her ear.

"Hello. Who's this? Oh, hi, Martha, I didn't recognize your voice. Sorry, Cassidy can't talk now. Yes, Buddy is here too. Sure, I'll give them both a message. Okay, that's kind of a strange message, but I'll tell them. See you tomorrow."

Delores dropped Cassidy's phone into her purse.

"What'd she say?" Cassidy asked.

"She sounded very cranky and gruff. She said to tell you both that tomorrow is going to be a day you'll never forget."

"I wonder what that's supposed to mean," Cassidy said.

I didn't know, but I sure didn't like the sound of it.

21

The first thing I did when I woke up the next morning was transform from Zane Tracy into Buddy Burger, alien superstar. I don't mean to sound stuck up or self-important with the superstar stuff, but on show day, when you're surrounded by cameras and the audience is waiting to see your every move, it's pretty exciting. It makes you feel like a superstar, that's for sure.

I went into the kitchen and gathered up all the remaining avocados ripening on the windowsill. There were about a dozen, which I figured would hold me until I could have Mary's guacamole at the lunch break. Eloise came shuffling down the hall in her pajamas and unicorn slippers, demanding that I pour her a special combination of her favorite cereals.

"I want half Cocoa Crunchies, a third Fruity Crisps, and the rest Wacky Cinnamon Puffs," she said. "With some chocolate sauce on the side."

"That's a powerful sugar binge," I said to her.

"I know." She laughed. "Just don't tell my mom."

"Don't tell your mom what?" a voice boomed from the hall. It was Delores coming to join us in her favorite leopard print robe.

"We don't want to tell you that we're planning a big surprise party for your birthday with cake and candles and everything," Eloise said.

"My birthday is a year away," Delores said.

"Well, it's never too soon to plan," I answered, grabbing my avocados and backing out of the kitchen. "You handle it from here," I whispered to Eloise as I left.

I was running late, so I decided to try to do two things at once. Instead of my usual long soak in the bathtub, I thought I'd take a shower and eat my avocados at the same time my body was getting hydrated. I grabbed a couple avocados, turned on the shower water, and stepped in.

We don't have showers on my planet, so it was a first for me. And let me take this opportunity to applaud you humans—the shower is one of your great inventions. My people invented the faster-than-light vehicle, but it doesn't hold a candle to the shower. I mean, the idea of warm water pounding down on your body while you just stand there and enjoy it is pure genius.

I loved the feeling of the shower water tumbling over the bumps on my head like a rushing brook racing over stones. Every now and then, I reached through the curtain and grabbed an avocado and took a bite, scooping out the soft flesh with one of my long fingernails. They were the perfect shape to scrape out every green little morsel stuck to the skin. I made a mental note that my newly discovered avocado-shower combo would be my weekly show-day ritual. It was the perfect way for an actor to prepare.

As we rode to the studio with Delores driving, Cassidy and I called Luis to remind him that show time was at six thirty that day, a half an hour earlier than usual. Duane felt that he needed extra time to shoot the talent show.

"No problem," Luis said on the speaker. "I'm done with

work at six. As soon as I can get that ridiculous Woody Woodpecker head off my face without scratching up my nose, I'll be there. You're going to break a leg with your song, Cass."

"What about my legs?" I asked. "I want to break them too."

"Everyone knows you're always a hit, Buddy. See you dudes later. I'll be in my usual seat in the front row."

We dropped off Eloise at the front door of her school. She had a mini-breakdown when her model skyscraper made of toilet paper slipped out of her hand and fell in a puddle. The windows she had carefully drawn with markers all ran together, making one big crazy window. As she cried, Delores got really annoyed, but Cassidy came to the rescue when she told Eloise it looked like she had built a skyscraper from outer space. That made Eloise happy again, and she picked up her soggy toilet rolls and skipped into school. I didn't think it was the right time to mention that I'd never seen a skyscraper like that on any planet I had ever visited.

When Delores let us off at the door of Stage 42, she told us she'd be back for the evening taping. She had a busy day of getting her fingernails done, her toenails done, her makeup done, and her eyebrows done. I'm not sure what was being done to any of those body parts, but I thought it was best not to ask.

Everyone is always work-focused on show day, so when

we walked onto the stage, you could feel the intensity. Mary was serving her special Friday French toast for breakfast (by the way, French toast is another of your human inventions that's right up there with the shower). Jules was handing out the final script changes. Duane was going over the short list with Beth on Camera Two. Rosa was hanging up the costumes in our dressing rooms. Tyler was getting his makeup done. He was always the first one in the makeup chair. Bruce, our makeup man, has to use a whole can of hair

spray to keep Tyler's hair looking like a movie star's. If you ask me, it looks more like a hair helmet, but then, no one asked me, especially not Tyler.

Ulysses was the only person on the stage messing around, which is good because he keeps everyone loose. He was going from person to person, showing them how he looked in his colonial three-cornered hat that he was going to wear for his Paul Revere impersonation in the talent show finale.

"One if by land, two if by lake," he yelled to Jamal, our camera man, taking off the hat and bowing.

"I think you got the body of water wrong," Jamal said. "I'm pretty sure it's two if by sea. But hey, you're close. I mean, water is water."

Cassidy and I waited for Duane to finish his conversation with Beth, then announced ourselves.

"We're here reporting for work," I said to Duane. "And in much better shape than yesterday."

"Good," he said, "because yesterday was a disaster."

"I practiced my song all night," Cassidy said. "And I found a new harmony I can't wait to try with Martha. Is she here yet?"

"Oh, good news," Duane said. "She called this morning, and she won't make it to rehearsal, but she'll be here at show time."

"What's so good about that?"

"She's at the doctor, getting treatment for her throat.

You know how terrible her voice sounded yesterday? The doctor is having Martha drink some concoction of vinegar and lemon, which she says will bring her voice back. And she's under orders to be absolutely silent until we shoot."

"Vinegar and lemon?" I said. "Yummy, that sounds delicious. Especially if you add some pickle relish."

"Buddy, you're the only person on Earth who would think that," Duane said. "But why am I surprised? Everything about you is weird. I guess that's why your fans love you."

"I'm worried about doing our song without one more rehearsal," Cassidy said.

"I wouldn't worry," Duane reassured her. "Martha's a trouper. You've always seen her rise to the occasion. Tonight will be no different. Once she feels the energy from the audience, she'll knock it out of the park."

We got to work and stayed focused all day. The dress rehearsal in the afternoon was a little bumpy, but Duane said that happens all the time. A bad dress rehearsal makes for a good performance. At dinner, I loaded up on the guacamole while everyone else heaped pasta and roast beef on their plates for energy. Then we all went to our dressing rooms to get into our costumes while the ushers guided the audience into the bleachers. I snuck out of my dressing room for a minute to peek at the audience, to make sure Luis was in the front row.

There he was, with his hair all slicked up and a Band-Aid on his nose from his Woody Woodpecker beak. He's so cool. He even looks good with a bandage on his nose.

On the way back to my dressing room, I knocked on Martha's door to make sure she was there.

"Whaaaat?" she shouted from inside. I guess the lemon-and-vinegar drink had worked, because her voice sure sounded strong to me.

"Just wishing you good luck," I hollered through the door. "See you out there."

"Oh, that you will," she hollered back. "I'll be there in all my glory."

The taping began with each of us being introduced to the audience. I did the special bow I had developed in which I wave and my sensory enhancer does too. I carry a Sour Patch candy in my pocket to make it come alive. Sometimes it even snorts, which the crowd goes wild for.

When Martha was introduced, she came out and stood next to me, but she didn't wave to the audience. She just stared at them with an unpleasant look on her face, her eyes reflecting the glow from the floodlights on the set. Fortunately, the moment passed quickly when Tyler swaggered out, hair helmet and all.

"I love you, Tyler," a girl in the front row screamed.

"I love me too." He grinned back at her.

The audience laughed and clapped. Everyone was in a great mood in anticipation of the show beginning.

Usually we shoot the script in order, but Duane wanted us to shoot the big musical number first, to keep the audience interested and fresh.

"I'm going to need to hear a lot of enthusiasm from you," Duane told the audience. "Your reactions are being recorded, and your participation is an important element of the show. If you like something, let the actors know. Okay, actors take your places, and let's shoot this thing."

I took my place on the riser in the center of the cafeteria set. Tyler sat down in the director's chair at the front edge of the set, his back to the audience. Cassidy and Martha waited in the wings.

"Talent show scene, take one," Jules called, holding up the black-and-white clacker in front of my face. With the sound of the clacker ringing in my ears, I heard Tyler say his first line.

"Action," he said, getting up from his director's chair to face the audience, his arm sweeping across his body with a grand flourish. I had never seen that gesture in rehearsal. I guess he was improvising. He was certainly making the most of his one word. I couldn't wait to see what he was going to do with "Cut!"

I got through the introduction of Cassidy and Martha without tripping over either of my tongues, then took my place on the side of the stage. When the girls came out and stepped up onto the riser, I noticed a scuffle between them. They were supposed to share the microphone, but Martha stepped in front of Cassidy so she could hog the entire thing. When Cassidy pushed back to get closer to the mic, Martha elbowed her hard in the ribs. Cassidy gasped, and while she was catching her breath, Martha picked up the mic and carried it off to the side of the stage. Cassidy couldn't believe what was happening and stood there, frozen and confused. I saw Jamal on Camera Three look over at Beth on Camera Two, as if to say, *Do you have any idea what's going on?* Beth just shrugged her shoulders.

Martha began to belt their song into the microphone, and it sounded screechy and awful, just like it had the day before. Suddenly, her mouth began to transform, growing bigger and bigger until it looked like it took up the whole bottom half of her face. As she held the mic and sang, she walked over to where I was standing on the set. Her eyes started to glow, first yellow and then a bright, burning gold. Wait a minute! I knew those eyes.

They were the eyes of Citizen Cruel.

My mind started to race as the puzzle pieces all snapped

together in my head. That wasn't truly Martha I was looking at. It was her body but inhabited by Citizen Cruel. She was a body snatcher, after all. The photographer, the spiky-haired guy at the party, the gas company inspector—they had all really been her, using other people's bodies to check me out, to gather information, to create her plan to capture me.

And now she had invaded Martha's body and was coming toward me, standing just inches away, her golden eyes flashing. Everyone else thought it was Martha.

I was the only one who knew the truth.

22

I **wanted to warn everyone. My mind was screaming,**
Run! Get out of here! There's an alien in our midst, and I
don't mean me.

But no sound came out of my mouth, only a gasp of terror as my three lungs filled with air.

I watched in horror as two beams of golden light shot out of Martha's eyes, growing brighter and brighter until they converged in a spinning circle. The circle whirled frantically like a tornado until it gradually slowed and I was able to make out a figure taking shape in the turbulent light.

The figure was Citizen Cruel, emerging from Martha's body and standing at her full height, towering over everyone on the stage, and laughing her raspy, awful laugh. Martha's vacant body dropped to the floor right at my feet and went limp. Her eyes were no longer golden, but they looked dazed and confused.

Everyone on the set held their breath, frozen in place, with no idea what was going on.

"Check that out," Ulysses yelled. "Her costume's just like Buddy's."

"Of course it is," Cassidy said. "Buddy always said he did a lot of research on his costume." She was a fast thinker.

The audience was transfixed. Not knowing any better, they thought this was part of the show.

I was totally confused, though. How could Citizen Cruel be standing there in front of me? I had personally put her in her spaceship and sent her into oblivion. Yet here she was, clutching her amulet with one hand and grabbing for me with the other.

"It's her!" Cassidy yelled, running to my side. "I thought we sent her away for good."

Cassidy reached for my hand, but Citizen Cruel pushed her away.

"You stupid earthling," she said. "If you had any brains, you would realize that I never left."

"But I started the engines myself!" I said.

"Starting is not finishing, Citizen Short Nose. You assumed that I took off. Assumptions are foolish."

"But you were unconscious."

"I wasn't unconscious for long. I took a Super Strength Blast from the Power Pole before I left for Earth, which allowed me to recover quickly enough to terminate the takeoff."

She tightened her grip around my neck so I could barely breathe.

"You have no choice now, Short Nose," she growled. "Either you come back with me willingly, or I will take you back piece by piece."

From the corner of my eye, I saw Luis hurtle over the railing and dash toward the stage. He was the only one, other than Cassidy and me, who knew there was a real alien threatening us.

Duane ripped off his headset and rushed onto the set too, yelling, "Cameras, keep rolling. This is good stuff. You okay, Martha?" he asked, kneeling down next to her.

"Sure, boss," she murmured, her eyes still rolled back in her head. "How was my song?"

"We did great," Citizen Cruel said. "It was a little cramped inside your body, but in the end, we stole the show. Or at least, I did."

Duane turned to Citizen Cruel and looked her up and down. "I don't know who you are or what kind of agent told you to crash our show," he said, "or even how you hid behind Martha, but you're one heck of an actress."

"She's not an actress," Cassidy screamed. "She's a body snatcher. She's dangerous!"

"I can confirm that," Luis shouted, diving at Citizen's Cruel's knees to try to bring her down. "Someone call the police. Or the FBI."

"Or the Bureau of Crazy Aliens," Ulysses said.

"Don't be cute," Luis shouted at him. "Call for help right now! I mean it!"

Citizen Cruel looked down at Luis, who was judo-chopping her behind the knees to try to make her collapse.

"You again!" she bellowed. "You pesky two-legged insect. Get out of my way—there's nothing you can do. Your boy is coming back with me where he belongs."

Citizen Cruel kicked Luis so hard, he flew into the air and landed flat on the cafeteria table with a thud. Then she lifted me up like a stuffed toy and slung me over her shoulder.

"Come on, you traitor, we have a nice jail pod waiting for you."

"Put him down right now," Cassidy yelled, stepping in front of her.

Citizen Cruel stared at her. The yellow beams from her eyes were so intense, Cassidy had to look away. "Don't take one step closer to me, or I'll snap him in half like a twig," she said.

"He's my best friend," Cassidy yelled defiantly. "You can't take him."

"Oh really? Who's going to stop me?"

"We are!" some kids in the audience yelled.

"Yeah, we are," the rest of the audience roared. "We love Buddy!"

In a grand motion, all three hundred members of the audience scrambled over the railing and rushed toward Citizen Cruel. Some grabbed her around the legs, some around her waist, and some attacked her arms. It looked like she was being swarmed by red ants.

"On the count of three, everybody pull in my direction!" Luis called out.

"You weaklings could never pull me down!" Citizen Cruel scoffed.

"One! Two!" Luis shouted.

Before he could even say "three," the audience members

tugged as if they were one giant person, and Citizen Cruel toppled over, hitting the floor with a booming crash that reverberated off the walls of the stage.

"Ulysses, where are the police?" Luis shouted.

"They're on the way."

"We have to hold her down until they get here," Cassidy ordered.

"We'll see about that," Citizen Cruel yelled back. "I'm stronger than all of you put together."

"Mary!" Cassidy shouted. "Do you have any strawberries left?"

"Not a one," Mary called back. "I used them all up at lunch."

"Okay, let's go to Plan B," I yelled. "Everybody sit on her like you're riding a horse. I saw that in a monster movie once, and it worked."

The kids in the audience thought this was really fun, like they were getting to participate in one of the stunt shows on the back lot. They climbed all over Citizen Cruel with no fear at all. That is, until she tried to kick her legs free and landed some serious blows on a few of them. She continued to kick and wave her arms furiously. It looked like the audience was riding a bucking bronco, with many falling off but enough holding on to keep her pinned down, at least temporarily. She was strong and a fighter, and I knew it was only a matter of time before she'd break free.

I looked around, trying desperately to think of a solution. And then I looked up and saw the solution staring me in the face.

"Luis, Cassidy, come with me," I hollered.

They followed me to the wall of the soundstage, where two ropes were attached to the metal pipes above us that held the lights.

"We need to grab the ropes and untie them from the wall so we can lower the pipes," I said.

"Why are we lowering the pipes?" Luis asked.

"No time to explain, just do it."

We lowered the metal pipe that was over the set until it was just above Citizen Cruel's head.

"That's good," I said. "Secure it to the wall."

Quickly, we tied the ropes down to keep the metal pipe in place. Then I grabbed one of the coiled cables that are used to connect the lights to the electricity box, and I tossed the second cable to Luis.

"Follow me," I told him and Cassidy.

We raced back to where Citizen Cruel was struggling on the floor to get free. I noticed Tyler cowering in the corner of the set, a look of terror on his face. He was the only one not helping.

"All right, everyone," I shouted. "We have to work together to slide these cables under her wrists and ankles. I need all hands on deck."

"She's not going to like that," Jamal said. "She's putting up a tremendous struggle."

"Struggle is good," Duane said. "The cameras are loving this. Keep going!"

Despite her flailing arms and legs, we were able to slide

the cables under Citizen Cruel's thick ankles. Getting them under her wrists proved to be more difficult. Every time anyone got near her, one of her hands would break free just long enough to swat them away.

"We need more help here," I called out. Rosa and Mary jumped in and tried to hold down her arms. But even then, Citizen Cruel was able to resist us.

"Tyler," I shouted out. "You're the only one not helping. You've got to do something."

"I don't do stunt work," he said. "I'm a serious actor."

"Ha!" Citizen Cruel exclaimed, managing to turn her head in his direction. "If you're so serious, why don't you have any lines. I'll tell you why. Because you're not good at anything."

"Oh yeah!" Tyler said, almost spitting with anger. "Watch this."

We all watched, wondering what he was going to do. Was he going to slug her in the face? Attack her with his bare hands? Twist those knobs on her neck until she cried for mercy?

Instead, he did a very Tyler thing. He ran to the makeup man, Bruce, pulled a can out of the plastic bag around his waist, and bolted over to Citizen Cruel.

"How's this!" he said, holding up the can and blasting

her in the face with hair spray. It stung her eyes and sent her into a fit of coughing, giving us the opportunity we needed to slip the cables around her wrists.

"Good thinking, Tyler," I said.

"Hair spray has always been my secret weapon," he gloated.

Now that the cables were wrapped around Citizen Cruel's ankles and wrists, we were ready to put my plan into action. Cassidy and I held the cable that was around her wrist, and Luis and Ulysses took her ankle cables. While everyone else held her down, we tied the cables onto the metal pipe just above her. When the knots were tightly secured, I commanded everyone who wasn't holding her to go to the ropes and help hoist her into the air.

There were at least ten of us at each of the two rope stations, all holding the rope and waiting for my command.

"When I say go, pull together with all your might!" I said. "GO!"

Everyone grunted and groaned, but working as a team, we were able to lift Citizen Cruel off the ground. Inch by inch, we raised her up until she was several feet from the floor, suspended in midair. No matter how she twisted and turned, she was stuck there, hanging from the pipe like a rotisserie chicken in the supermarket.

"You won't get away with this," she bellowed. "My planet will send backup to destroy each and every one of you."

"We've heard enough from you," Tyler said, jumping on one of the cafeteria chairs and reaching up to his full height to blast her again with another shot of hair spray.

"That should keep her quiet for a while." He smirked. "I use extra hold, you know."

While her vision was blurred, I took the opportunity to sneak up to Citizen Cruel and yank the amulet from around her neck.

"I need that," she said.

"And that's exactly why I'm taking it. You're not getting away this time."

She laughed her chicken-bone cackle. "You are so wrong. I have powers you haven't even dreamed of. I'm not done with you."

Cassidy had come to find me, and she overheard this part of the conversation.

"Buddy, she's scaring me," Cassidy said.

"She's all talk," I said, trying to reassure Cassidy of something I wasn't sure of myself.

As we stepped away from Citizen Cruel to rejoin the group, I heard her murmur, "I'll be back when you least expect it."

Duane was happier than I had ever seen him.

"Cut!" he called out.

"Hey," Tyler said. "That's my line."

With Tyler's movie star smile spreading across his face, he gestured broadly with his arm and shouted, "Cut!" It's too bad the cameras had already stopped rolling, because for once, he did a really good job.

"None of that was in the script," Duane said, "but we got ourselves one fabulous scene. Thanks, everyone. I can hardly wait to edit this together and see what we've got. I don't think anything this sensational has ever been on TV."

Even though the soundstage was supposed to be sound-proof, there was no mistaking the wail of police sirens as squad cars arrived from all directions. When we saw the police officers rush through the door, the cast and crew and the three hundred members of the audience all cheered.

Citizen Cruel had been defeated and evil had been over-powered by a bunch of plain, old regular humans and one teenage alien.

23

When the police realized that they had a real alien on their hands, they called in their special operations unit, who called the FBI, and before you knew it, Stage 42 was swarming with people wearing black tactical gear. The FBI brought in an armored eighteen-wheeler truck, and it took at least fifty officers to load Citizen Cruel into its secured container. As they carried her across the soundstage, still hanging from our pipe, she shouted at them in our home planet language. I won't translate what she said—it was that bad.

"Where are you taking her?" I asked the police captain.

"The FBI has places for creatures like that," he said.

"Where?"

"Top secret. No one knows for sure. All I can tell you is it's somewhere in America, it's underground, and it's surrounded by mountains. And filled with scientists taking notes."

"And you're sure it's a secure place where she can't escape? Because she's a shapeshifter and a body snatcher, this one. No one should get too close to her."

"Oh, don't worry. It's maximum security to the max. Nothing that has gone in there has ever come out."

"That's good to know," I said, finally breathing a sigh of relief.

"Oh, and by the way," the captain went on, "my kids watch you on *Oddball Academy*. They love you and especially that thing on the back of your costume. Come to think of it, your costume looks a lot like that real alien."

"Yes," I said, repeating Cassidy's explanation. "I did a lot of research to get it as real as possible."

This was clearly a dangerous topic, and I wanted to get away from it as fast as I could, so I offered to take a video with him for his kids. He was thrilled.

"Hey, kids, it's me, Dad," he said into his cell phone camera. "Look who I'm with. Buddy, say something to Lydia and Mason in alien."

I had to think fast, because if I spoke my own language, it would sound exactly like Citizen Cruel, so instead, I spoke the most alien language I know—Hungarian.

"*As tollomban nincs tinta*," I said, waving and smiling for the kids. That means "my pen has no ink." It actually wasn't true; my pen was full of ink. But as I've told you before, my Hungarian is not good, and it's one of the only sentences I can say.

A week later, when the episode of *Oddball Academy* with Citizen Cruel aired on TV, the whole cast and crew had a viewing party at Cassidy's house. Delores served carrots and celery sticks with onion dip for us and no dip for Cassidy.

We settled in to watch the show. It was amazing. Martha was embarrassed that her voice sounded so awful in her song, but we all reassured her that she did the best she could with an alien inside her. Tyler thought his performance was worthy of a "best actor" award.

"Even though I only had two words, they were magnificent," he claimed with his usual modesty.

The part where the audience attacked Citizen Cruel was more exciting than I even remembered. She may be the cruelest thing to ever live, but I have to admit, she's very photogenic—the camera loves her.

Later that night, we learned that the episode got the highest rating of our season, and the network executives were ecstatic. I even got a call from the network president, Barbara Daniel, who said they wanted to change my billing from costar to the star of the show. We talked for a few minutes, while Cassidy and her mom were serving cheese-burger sliders, each garnished with a tiny pickle, to the guests. Luis had brought a tub of grandmother's guacamole as a special treat for me. I kept my eyes on it as I talked on the phone.

After I hung up, I bolted for the guacamole, but Cassidy stopped me in my tracks to find out what the call was about.

"Oh, Ms. Daniel called to say the ratings went through

the roof," I said. "We got the highest ratings for our time period in four years."

"That's amazing," Cassidy said. "What else did she say?"

"Well, she said they got so many comments about me that she wants me to be billed as the star of the show from now on."

"Oh wow, that's amazing too," Cassidy said, with a little less enthusiasm. "I mean, it's great for you. Weird for me, but great for you."

"It's not going to be weird at all, Cass, because I said no."

"Buddy, you said no to top billing?"

"I sure did. I told her that I wouldn't be where I am without you and that I could never take your place. I told her I would be honored if we costarred together."

"You said that?"

"Not only did I say it, I learned it from you. Friends support friends no matter what. We're in this together."

Cassidy threw her arms around me and gave me a hug.

"Oh, Buddy," she said, "You're the best space creature I've ever met."

I looked at the cast and crew gathered around the living room. I had made a life for myself on Earth, and these people were my family.

I was one lucky alien.

24

Deep in the heart of America, in a secret underground laboratory known to only a few, Citizen Cruel sat in her cramped concrete cube. Had anyone been able to hear, they would have noticed the scrapping sound of her long sharp fingernail as it scratched away layers of the concrete wall. It was a small hole she was boring, only big enough to allow a tiny beam of light to penetrate the darkness.

But it was a beginning . . .

ACKNOWLEDGMENTS

We are grateful to everyone at Abrams Kids, especially our leader, Andrew Smith, our editor, Maggie Lehrman, and the entire Abrams team for helping us bring *Alien Superstar* to life. And of course, we send much respect to our talented illustrator, Ethan Nicolle, who brought Buddy C. Burger and his two worlds into dramatic focus. We are both thankful for our careers in television, especially all the creative talented people who populated our lives on the soundstage. This book is an homage to them.

To our agents, Esther Newberg, Ellen Goldsmith-Vein, and Eddie Gamarra, thank you for being champions of this book and of all the books we've written together since we started our collaboration. A special thank-you to Theo Baker, our advisor in all things alien. Finally, we thank all of our readers who, since 2003, have supported our vision and shown us their hearts.

Henry Winkler and Lin Oliver
Hollywood, 2020

ABOUT THE AUTHORS

Henry Winkler is an Emmy Award–winning actor, writer, director, and producer who has created some of the most iconic TV roles, including the Fonz in *Happy Days* and Gene Cousineau in *Barry*.

Lin Oliver is a children's book writer and a writer and producer for both TV and film. She is currently the executive director of the Society of Children's Book Writers and Illustrators (SCBWI).

They both live in Los Angeles, California.